JUST FRIENDS

BOOK 3 OF THE *JOHNSON FAMILY* SERIES

DELANEY DIAMOND

Delaney Diamond
Atlanta, Georgia

ISBN-13: 978-1-940636-13-9

Chapter One

Pumping his hips, Trenton Johnson gazed down at Tonya, the beautiful young woman beneath him. A thin coat of sweat covered his body in the dark, where only a sliver of light managed to maneuver its way between the thick curtains covering the windows in her bedroom. He had her wrists pinned together above her head and one hand lifted her hips to accept each of his powerful thrusts. Her cries of passion filled the bedroom.

"You like that?" he panted.

"Yes, Trenton! Yesss!" Almost there, tension vibrated in her voice, and his own release pressed ever closer.

Using steady, rhythmic pumps, he sent them both to orgasmic completion. She released a gasping wail, and his body shuddered before collapsing on top of her. With a groan, Trenton rolled onto his back, panting heavily. Needing a few minutes to recover, he ran a hand over his damp face and stared up at the rotating ceiling fan.

"Incredible," Tonya moaned, finally catching her breath. Limber and enthusiastic, she had turned into one of his regular hookups from the first night he'd dived between her silky brown thighs. He'd be ready for round two soon.

Right then, his phone rang, a special ring tone he never ever ignored. Trenton stretched across the mattress and picked up the phone from the table next to the bed. "Hello?"

"I'm at home. You still coming over?" Alannah asked.

His best friend was back in town. Trenton smiled. "Of course."

"When are you coming?"

"Soon."

"How soon?"

"Soon."

"You busy?"

He glanced at Tonya, whose frowning gaze held a healthy dose of curiosity. "A little bit."

"*Oh*," she said, the word heavy with meaning. "I'll see you when you get here, then. Bring me something to eat when you do."

"All right. Bye." Trenton replaced the phone on the bedside table and rolled onto his back.

"Who was that?" Tonya pouted.

When he didn't answer, she stroked his bicep and, resting her head on his shoulder, flung one shapely leg across his thighs. An obvious ploy to get him to relax.

Trenton stirred, disentangling himself from her brown limbs, and she moaned her discontent. "I need to get rid of this." He indicated the condom with a pointing finger.

"Hurry back," she replied lazily, with a languid stretch.

He closed the door to the bathroom and disposed of the condom in the toilet, relieved himself, and then flushed.

Staring at his reflection in the mirror while washing his hands, he thought about Tonya. She had a nice face and great figure, and they'd been lovers on and off for eight months, ever since she'd popped out of the cake at his fraternity brother's bachelor party. But they didn't have much in common besides sexual gymnastics, and he was bored. Probably time to move on.

He re-entered the bedroom and picked up his discarded clothes from the floor.

"I thought you were staying, for another round," Tonya said quietly.

"Nah, I better go." Trenton tugged on his boxer briefs.

"Why?" She sat up and let the sheet fall to her waist. "You can stay the night if you want."

"I have things to do. Have to go see a friend of mine." He

slipped the polo shirt over his head.

Only the rustle of his clothes could be heard in the quiet that followed. Then, "Alannah."

She said the name with a heavy amount of resentment, and Trenton bristled but slipped on his shoes.

"What is it with her? What makes her so special?"

His head snapped up, and he looked Tonya squarely in the eye. "I don't like your tone."

She shrank back against the headboard. "I didn't mean anything by it. It's just..."

Definitely time for him to move on. The cracks in their perfectly orchestrated relationship were starting to show. They'd had some great times—excellent, *freaky* times. He turned an eye to the cuffs abandoned on the floor.

But if he didn't end this now, it could get out of hand. He'd been in a situation before where he stayed in a sexual relationship past its shelf life, and there was nothing pretty about a woman who thought she deserved more than he offered. And he sure as hell wouldn't tolerate anyone trying to come between him and his best friend.

Trenton picked up his phone and keys from the nightstand, and Tonya slipped naked from the bed. Pressing her supple body against his, she kissed his bicep, where the image of a hissing snake circled the muscle—one of many tattoos that ran the length of both arms.

"See you next week?" She looked up at him with a hopeful expression on her face and placed a hand on the waistband of his jeans.

He'd have his executive assistant send her flowers and a nice piece of jewelry. Expensive trinkets softened the blow and minimized the dramatic fallout of the untimely end to an affair.

He extricated himself from her arms. "I'll call you."

****

Trenton parked his white, customized Range Rover in the driveway outside the two-bedroom townhouse Alannah rented. Like the others in the complex, it had an attached one-car garage. All of them, painted in bright, candy-colored paint and white trim, looked like a row of dollhouses in the daytime, each with a perfect little square of grass that was so well maintained and nurtured, it looked like an area rug had been dropped in front of the house.

On the way over he'd stopped at The Best Thai Restaurant, a fitting name. It really was the best, and the only Thai restaurant he and Alannah patronized.

Two weeks had passed since he'd last seen his buddy. She'd used her vacation to visit her parents in Arizona, where they'd moved after her father retired from the post office and her mother from teaching. Fourteen days had never felt so long, and he couldn't wait to see her.

Trenton strolled up the stone-lined walkway to the unit, second from the left in a building that held four houses. He rang the doorbell, and when Alannah swung open the door, his chest expanded and he couldn't suppress the grin that spread across his face. Seeing her always filled him with such excitement, as if he'd won the lottery.

"Hey, stranger. What's that?" She reached for the bag.

He held the plastic sack out of reach. "Is that all I'm good for? Come here, girl. I missed you."

He grabbed her with one arm and lifted her from the floor. He inhaled her candy-apple smell, the scent of the sanitizer she often used.

Giggling softly, she wound her arms around his neck and squeezed him tight. The best hugs in the world came from his buddy.

"Glad to know I was missed," she said softly.

He set her back on the floor and closed the door. "You know you were missed."

Alannah stood before him in a pair of gray gym shorts and a white tank top with her hair hidden under a burgundy satin bonnet. She frowned at him. "I go away for two weeks and you let yourself go."

Trenton rubbed a hand across his bearded jaw. "See what happens when you leave me? I'm lost without you."

She ran a hand over his head. "You need a haircut badly."

"Careful now." He brushed a hand over the top of his head. "Wouldn't want you to get seasick from all these waves."

"Oh lord. These women have your head so swollen, I'm

surprised you made it through the door."

He chuckled and eyed the bonnet on her head. "You're ready for bed?"

"I didn't know if you'd be staying late with one of your hoes."

"I told you I'd be here as soon as you let me know you were home. And by the way, I don't mess with hoes."

"If you say so, but I figured I'd better get ready for bed anyway." Her eyes lit up and a sneaky smile curved her lips. "And I have a surprise for you. But before I tell you my surprise…" She sniffed the air and eyed the bag in his hand. "I smell Thai."

This time she managed to snatch the bag, and he laughed as she scurried off in the direction of the kitchen. He trailed her to the pint-sized space decorated with mahogany cabinets and stainless steel appliances. Her home had an open floor plan, with the kitchen, dining area—made up of a small round table and four chairs with off-white covers—and living room bleeding right into each other.

"Lemonade?" Alannah asked.

"Sounds good." Trenton leaned against the counter near the sink while Alannah removed the contents of the bag onto the breakfast bar. Eyeing the row of twenty-odd recipe books of various sizes nestled on the shelf above the microwave, he said, "You added to your collection."

She nodded. "I picked up two cookbooks on Southwest cooking when I was in Arizona." She removed two plates from the cabinets and placed them on the Formica counter.

"How was Arizona?" They'd talked a few times while she was gone, but for the most part he'd left her alone to enjoy her time off.

"Nothing special. My sisters flew in the last few days, so the whole family spent time together. We had a blast." She inhaled deeply. "This smells so good. Who cooked? Aat or Chayo?"

Their favorite chef was Aat. They always increased the tip in the jar at the register whenever he cooked. The meals were hit or miss when Chayo worked in the kitchen.

"Aat, and when he found out you were back in town, he threw in extra basil rolls. He's in love with you."

She laughed, tossing a glance at him over her shoulder. "Stop."

"He is. If you ever show him the slightest interest, I'm sure he'll leave his wife." He watched her pull utensils from drawers and then start scooping out brown rice. "So, what's my surprise?" he asked.

She turned to face him, and her hazel eyes met his hesitantly. "I've been doing some thinking. I'm not getting any younger."

"None of us are."

"And…well, I want to make some changes in my life. So…you know what, it's better for me to show you than tell you." She removed the bonnet from her head and released her hair. Running her fingers through the strands, she sifted them loose until they tumbled past her shoulders. "What do you think?"

Trenton took a good look at her. He walked over and lifted a few soft strands and rubbed them between his fingers. "You colored it."

"Yes." Alannah bit the inside of her bottom lip. "What do you think?"

"I like it," he said slowly. The vibrant auburn brightened her light amber skin tone. "Brings more attention to your freckles." Rust-colored spots lay splattered across her nose and cheeks. He grinned and tweaked her nose.

She slapped his hand away. "Really? Ugh." She hated her freckles, but he thought they were cute. She turned around so he could see her hair from the back and pushed her fingers through the shiny strands, shaking her head so the thick mass rippled back and forth across her back. "I had it cut in layers, too." Turning back around, she said, "I know it's pretty drastic. Well, for me it's drastic, but I only had a few inches cut off. The craziest thing is the color. Auburn. Can you believe it? After having dull brown hair all my life, I went with auburn." Her eyes brightened and filled with the excitement of the change.

"It's an attention getter," Trenton said evenly. "Hey, where are your glasses?" Being nearsighted, she seldom went without her glasses. Every time she took them off, she walked around squinting.

"Oh, that's the other thing." She pointed to her eyes. "Contacts."

"Contacts?"

"Yes. I have the long-wearing ones that you can sleep in. It took me a while to get used to them. Sometimes I still reach for my glasses and then realize they aren't there. It's crazy, but yep, I'm wearing contacts now. I've had them for a week already."

Trenton scratched the back of his head. "I don't understand. What's going on with you? What's with all the changes?"

Alannah shrugged and started spooning food onto the plates again. "Like I said, I'm not getting any younger. It's time for me to act and look like a woman."

"I liked the way you looked before."

She smiled briefly at him over her shoulder. "That's sweet, but you're saying that cause you're my friend. I want to know what a man thinks."

"I'm a man." What the hell?

She giggled on her way to the refrigerator. "You know what I mean. You're more like a girlfriend than a man."

Trenton stiffened. Since when?

As Alannah poured lemonade—hers was good and tart because she made it with fresh lemons and none of that powdered stuff—into two glasses, he paid closer attention to her. She didn't just look different, she was acting different. She displayed more confidence than usual. And the shorts had to be the shortest pair of shorts he'd ever seen her wear. They put her legs on display in a way that made him take notice. Had her legs always been that long?

She was small up top but thick on the bottom, and the contrast was never more noticeable than today. Her butt appeared round and full, and her hips looked as if they'd widened since he'd seen her last. Not likely, but still.

Dayum.

"No comment?" Alannah handed him a glass of lemonade.

Trenton blinked. "About what?"

"About everything. My new look?" Her voice fell off into a soft, disappointed whisper. She'd expected a different reaction, and for the life of him he couldn't figure out why he wasn't excited for her.

"You look nice. I mean, you know, it's different. The changes will take some getting used to." Trenton took a large swig of lemonade, wishing the glass contained something stronger.

She nodded and handed him a plate of brown rice, seafood with panang curry, and three basil rolls.

"Hey." He stepped closer, studying her downturned face. "You took me by surprise, but you look really nice." This change couldn't have been easy for her to make. She wasn't the kind of person to bring attention to herself. She preferred to be quiet and in the background, so auburn hair really was a drastic change.

"You're not just saying that?" She looked up at him with uncertainty.

"From one girlfriend to the other, I'm not just saying that." He grinned and she grinned back. "Come on, let's go watch that movie you promised me. It better not be a foreign film, either."

"You liked the last one," she said, following him into the living room.

"Just because I liked it doesn't mean I want to see that mess all the time."

She sighed dramatically. "This one is a South Korean thriller."

He groaned. "So I have to read subtitles?"

"Oh my goodness. What a horror. You have to read."

"That mouth of yours is going to get you into serious trouble one day."

Plates in hand, they piled onto the sofa and set the drinks on the table closest to Trenton. Alannah folded her legs beneath her and turned on the television. A few presses of the remote and the opening scene rolled out, immediately capturing their attention with an explosion.

Trenton forked a shrimp into his mouth. He chewed slowly, ruminating on Alannah's altered appearance. "What brought on all these changes? Are you really worried about getting older?"

"Well…"

Her hesitation caught his attention. "Well what? Are you seeing someone?" He stared at her.

"No." She ducked her head and her hair fell forward, hiding her face so he couldn't see all her features.

"Are you sure that's a no, or do you really mean yes?"

Discomfort set up residence in his stomach. She hadn't mentioned she was seeing anyone, and if she was, he'd certainly never seen her go to all this trouble for a man before.

Alannah moved rice around on her plate with the fork. "I'm not seeing anyone, but there is a guy at work. I don't know…he's attractive and seems nice." She shrugged.

"What guy? I didn't know there was a guy." They told each other everything, but she'd been holding out on him.

"It's not a big deal. He doesn't work in my department. I noticed him, that's all. And I think he already has a girlfriend, anyway." She bit into a basil roll, the crispy vegetables crunching between her teeth.

"Do I know him?" He'd been to her job plenty of times and knew a lot of her coworkers.

"No," she said shortly.

"Hold up, what's going on?" Trenton set his plate on the glass coffee table. "If your mystery man is with someone, why are you going through all these changes?"

She sighed. "Can we watch the movie, please?"

"No." Trenton picked up the remote and paused the movie.

She shot him an annoyed look.

"Talk to me."

Alannah gave him the silent treatment and stared at the TV screen.

"What happened in Arizona?" Trenton asked.

She tilted her face away from him, again keeping her expression hidden.

"Hey." Trenton grasped her chin and forced her head back around to him. "What's going on, Lana? What happened? Did somebody hurt you?" The thought of anyone hurting her filled him with rage. One hand clenched into a fist, and he leaned in, paying close attention to her body language.

She shook her head. "Nobody hurt me, and nothing happened in Arizona. It's…everything, Trent. I'm tired of being me. I want to be noticed." Watery eyes looked up at him.

"What's this?" Trenton took her plate and placed it beside his. Then he pulled her into his arms and she pressed her face into his chest. "There's nothing wrong with you, knucklehead."

She sniffled and swiped a tear from her cheek. "I know there's nothing wrong with me—not anything major, but I want to stand out."

"Well, auburn hair will do it," he said. She lightly punched him in the stomach and he laughed, giving her an affectionate squeeze. "It's a compliment, dipshit."

"Promise?"

"Promise. I like the color."

"Terri suggested it," Alannah said, referring to one of her close girlfriends.

He had reservations about her friend's influence but kept the comment to himself. He kissed the top of her head. A new scent. Liking it, he smiled a little and took a bigger whiff.

"Your hair smells different."

"I'm trying a new shampoo. It's honeysuckle scented."

Trenton took another whiff. He really liked that scent. Stroking her hair, he asked, "Nobody messed with you, though, right?"

"No, Trent." She sat up and away from him, breathing heavily, an annoyed sound. "I'm not eight years old anymore. You don't have to keep protecting me."

His throat closed up, and the discomfort he'd experienced earlier reappeared and filled all the corners of his stomach. He'd always been there. For twenty-two years, they'd always been there for *each other.* He didn't know any other way to behave.

"That's bullshit. We have each other's back."

Her shoulders slumped. "I know," she said quietly.

He took her hand, rubbing a thumb over the slenderness of her wrist and the delicate, narrow fingers. "We look out for each other. That's what we do."

"Yeah." Her upper lip trembled but she forced a smile. "Best friends forever," she said, repeating the mantra they'd said for years.

"Forever," he confirmed. He squeezed her hand.

Instead of happiness, Trenton thought he saw sadness in the depths of her eyes. But before he could properly analyze the emotion, she averted her gaze, picked up her plate, and restarted the movie.

"Yay, I'm really looking forward to reading this movie," he grumbled.

Alannah rolled her eyes. "Give it a chance," she said, past a mouthful of seafood.

He picked up his own plate, set his feet on the coffee table, and reclined against the back of the sofa.

But Alannah's minor meltdown stayed with him for a long time after the movie started. Every now and again he watched her from the corner of his eye. She appeared normal enough, back to her old self, yet he suspected she hadn't told him everything. The makeover and what she'd said worried him. He had a feeling even bigger changes were coming.

And he wasn't going to like a single one of them.

Chapter Two

Alannah put away the dishes and then walked quietly back to the living room where Trenton was fast asleep. After the South Korean flick they'd watched a full episode of *Law & Order*, but fifteen minutes into the second episode she'd glanced over and saw his eyes were closed.

Despite being a member of one of the wealthiest families in America, no one could ever accuse Trenton of being a snob. His total lack of pretentiousness wasn't limited to his friendships, and even extended to the clothes he wore. Tonight, for example, he'd dressed down in a simple polo shirt and jeans, and it wasn't uncommon to see him do something as unorthodox as pair a department store shirt under a Brunello Cucinelli jacket.

As Alannah watched his six-foot-three body loll on the sofa, legs outstretched and head resting on the back of the chair, she smiled. Full lips, way too luscious for a man, were partially open in the deep throes of sleep. She should take a picture and blackmail him with it, but even in this comical pose, he managed to be endearing and was still the most attractive man she'd ever laid eyes on. Sexy and with an abundance of testosterone, he had an impressive build of lean, taut muscles that traversed his body from top to bottom.

His height could be imposing, particularly since she was a full nine inches shorter than him, but there was nothing threatening about Trenton. He smiled too often and had an arrestingly beautiful and friendly face that made him well liked and put people at ease. In fact, he couldn't stand to see anyone upset and was that rare type of person beloved by both men and women. He'd even figured out how to remain friends with his exes, including the ones who swore undying love to him.

Her gaze skimmed his wide shoulders and the colorful tattoos staining his muscular arms like shirtsleeves, hidden under pricey suits Monday through Friday but today fully exposed because of the navy-blue polo shirt. Dark jeans hugged muscular thighs and long legs that strode with confidence wherever he went. And his big, masculine hands easily swallowed hers every time he'd ever taken her hand in his.

Alannah bit down on the inside of her bottom lip, fighting back the soul-crushing longing of wanting to touch him the way his lovers could. What did his mouth taste like? What would it feel like to have his powerful body take possession of hers?

Between her legs tingled from the arousing thoughts and she closed her eyes. She'd never know. Why even allow her mind to go in that direction, where she dwelt on her pathetic feelings and desires for her best friend? She'd had plenty of time to think, and she intended to carry out her plan. Boring, quiet Alannah was a person of the past. Exciting, sexy Alannah would make a splash in Seattle and date up a storm.

She walked over to the sofa and shook Trenton's shoulder. His head popped up, eyes fluttering open. They were a brilliant green color, the same shade as English peas or the fresh blades of grass that emerged in the spring. The pupils appeared hazy and then focused on her as he came fully awake.

"I fell asleep?" He stifled a yawn.

"For a little while."

"I better get out of here."

He stretched as he stood, reminding her of a mountain lion—big, golden, and powerful. He even moved like the dangerous predator, with an economy of motion that suggested he was never in a hurry, but always ready to pounce on prey. She envied the women lucky enough to be his victims.

"If you're tired, sleep in the guest room," Alannah offered.

Trenton shook his head and rubbed his hairy jaw. "I need to head home. I'm going to the club to play squash at eight." With a big yawn, he trudged toward the door.

She followed, ogling the way the jeans hugged his tight butt, and stifled a sigh.

Trenton turned with his hand on the knob. "I'm going to dinner at Mother's tomorrow night. You coming? I can swing by and pick you up."

"Can't. I have a full day tomorrow. I have a million things to do before I go back to work on Monday."

"Adelina's cooking a traditional Mexican meal." Adelina was his mother's housekeeper who'd been with her for many years. "Do you understand what that means? Chicken mole is on the menu. You cannot, under any circumstances, miss authentic chicken mole."

Alannah laughed. His sense of humor was one of the many things she loved about him. "Yes, I understand, but I have to pass. I really can't make it."

Trenton placed a hand on each of her shoulders. The heat from his touch singed through her clothes to the skin underneath. She wished he would touch her, just once, in an inappropriate way.

He searched her face. "You're all right, aren't you?"

"Of course." She smiled brightly to put his mind at ease. "I had a weird moment earlier, but I'm fine. And of course you know I'd come if I didn't have a million things to do, which includes picking up Angel from the kennel."

At the mention of her brown and black Yorkshire terrier, Trenton wrinkled his nose in disgust and dropped his hands. He'd given her the dog as a Christmas present several years ago after she'd fallen in love with a mutual friend's dog.

"You should leave her there," he said.

"You say things like that and wonder why she hates you." The dog growled and barked at Trenton every time he came over. Oddly enough, she only behaved that way toward him. With everyone else, she was loving and playful.

"Like I care what that damn dog thinks."

Trenton pulled her into a hug. She pressed her face into his neck and inhaled the crisp, herbal fragrance of his cologne and the fresh, right-out-of-the-shower scent of his skin. He must have stopped at home before coming over.

The hair on his jaw tickled her face, but she resisted the urge to rub her cheek against the rough texture. His strong arms held her close, and she longed to run her hands up under his shirt and spread them across his wide back.

Releasing her, he said, "I'm out of here. Sleep tight. I'll see you next week for lunch?"

She wanted to say no, that she couldn't take the lunches and the dinners and the movies anymore. Instead, she said, "I'll let you know."

He tilted his head sideways, frowning. "You're canceling lunch?"

"I'm not canceling, but I don't know what my schedule will be like yet. Things are probably backed up at the lab, so I'll have to see before I confirm lunch."

"Call me Monday night and let me know."

"Okay." Agreeing was easier than fighting. "And please get a haircut and shave. Next time I see you, I don't want you to look like a mountain man."

With a playful gleam in his eye, he grinned. "I don't know, I might let my hair grow a little longer. And the ladies like the beard." He scrubbed his cheek with his knuckles.

"With that big head of yours, will you be able to make it through the front door to your truck?"

He chuckled heartily as he left, and Alannah closed the door behind him and let out a sigh.

"I didn't hear the deadbolt," Trenton said on the other side of the door.

She rolled her eyes and twisted the bolt to the right. "Happy now?"

"Yes, smart ass. Good night."

Alannah smiled a little and stood at the door until she heard him drive away. After retrieving the satin bonnet from the kitchen, she turned out the lights and climbed the stairs to the second floor.

She entered the quiet sanctuary of her bedroom, which contained silver and lavender furnishings and a large window with matching curtains that faced the front of the house. When she'd moved in, she asked Trenton to help her paint the room and put together the white dresser, bureau, and night stand she'd purchased from IKEA. He'd shown up that Saturday with workers in tow and whisked her off to lunch and a movie. By the time they'd returned, the furniture had been put together and the room painted white with a heather-gray accent wall.

Alannah grinned as she stripped off her clothes. She'd only been teasing when she'd made that request of Trenton. As down to earth as he was, he did not like manual labor.

She pulled a spaghetti-strapped top over her head and then dug out a pair of Trenton's striped silk boxers that, unbeknownst to him, she'd pilfered from his dresser. Over the years, she'd borrowed T-shirts that she'd never returned, but she'd also stolen from him—mostly boxers, but the occasional dress shirt and tie had also made its way to the bottom of her dresser drawer. If he ever saw her collection, he'd think she was a sicko for sure.

She slipped into the queen-size bed and turned out the light, but Trenton filled her thoughts. She deserved at least an Emmy nod for effectively hiding her feelings. While she wanted to be more than friends, she was firmly, unequivocally in the Friend Zone and had been for over twenty years. That would never change, and she winced as the pain of resignation lanced through her chest.

For one, she wasn't his type. Too quiet and not sexy enough. Second, when two people have been friends as long as she and Trenton had been, it was too risky to take a chance on ruining their stable relationship.

Alannah pulled the covers over her head and curled into a tight, miserable ball.

The Friend Zone was a place she'd come to despise. Because Trenton was the complete package. Everything a woman could want. He had a great personality, a sense of humor, was confident, and very good-looking.

Unfortunately, he was her best friend, closest confidant, and she was hopelessly in love with him.

Chapter Three

Alannah removed her lab coat and hung it in her locker at DymoGenesis, the biomedical engineering facility where she worked. As a researcher in tissue engineering, she and the other employees in the fourth-floor lab worked on the creation of artificial organs and researched the effect they had on the human body.

"I love your new look," one of her coworkers whispered as she zipped behind her.

"Thanks." Alannah smiled shyly. The new hairstyle and clothes had caused an uptick in her workplace popularity, and she still wasn't used to all the attention yet.

She hadn't brought her lunch today, and suffering through paltry choices of mystery meat and overcooked pasta in the company cafeteria didn't appeal, so she decided to take advantage of the sunny weather and go out for lunch. She exited the building into the University District, an eclectic mix of historic homes, eateries, and shops that surrounded the University of Washington. Strolling down University Way, or "The Ave," as Seattleites tended to call it, she chose a sandwich shop for lunch. She planned to sit at one of the outside tables and peruse the fashion magazine tucked into her purse to get ideas for her next outfits.

Minutes later, she settled on a bench with a hot pastrami

sandwich, chips, and a drink. She'd only taken one bite of the sandwich and hadn't even removed the magazine from her purse yet when a male voice asked, "Mind if I join you?"

Alannah looked up into the smiling and very attractive face of her coworker, Connor Bodell. Tall and lanky with dirty blond hair, he'd caused quite a tizzy among the researchers when hired months ago.

Alannah's mouth fell open, but she didn't know what to say. Another empty table was only a few feet away, and she wondered why he didn't sit there instead.

Finally, she found her voice. "Sure. No one's sitting there." Inclining her head, she indicated the empty bench on the other side of the table.

"Thanks." He sat down. "I'm Connor, by the way."

"Alannah."

He unwrapped his chicken sandwich and squeezed ketchup onto the edge of the wax paper. "So you work on the fourth floor at DymoGenesis, right?" He took a bite of his sandwich.

"Yes. And you're in...administration?"

She knew exactly which department he worked in. Everyone did—the women, anyway.

Connor nodded and swallowed. "Quality control department."

"Boo. Hiss. Should I even be talking to you?"

"Of course. I help you do your job better." He grinned, and his eyes lit up. They were green, like Trenton's, but a lighter shade.

Alannah glanced down at her chips, silently berating herself. She had a bad habit of comparing every man she met to Trenton. No point, when he remained in a class by himself.

"I've been trying to work up the nerve to talk to you," Connor said.

Startled, Alannah shifted her gaze across the table. "Me?"

He laughed softly. "Yes, you. Why do you sound so surprised?"

"I...I guess because I am surprised. I thought you were interested in someone else."

She and some of the other female employees had speculated about his relationship with a chemist on the second floor. They'd had lunch together in the cafeteria a few times, and one evening when she'd worked late, Alannah had spotted them chatting out by his car in the parking lot. That was when she'd lost all hope of ever being noticed by him. But that had been weeks ago, before her trip to Arizona. Now that she thought about it, she hadn't seen them together since her return.

"Well, you're wrong. I've had my eye on you since I started working at DymoGenesis."

Not accustomed to this kind of attention, Alannah felt heat rise in her cheeks. "Oh." She munched a chip, unable to think of anything else to say.

"I'm not saying it to flatter you. It's the truth," Connor said quietly. He set down his sandwich, and his expression became more earnest. "I didn't approach because you always seemed so quiet. I wondered if you'd even be interested in a guy like me."

"A guy like you? What does that mean?"

"I'm not exactly a brainiac."

Alannah laughed softly. "I'm not only interested in smart men."

"No?"

"No." Her heart rate sped up a little, and she bit the inside of her bottom lip. *Oh my goodness, where is this going?*

"So, I have a chance?" He dipped a fry in ketchup and looked up at her right before slipping it into his mouth.

"I would say so."

He nodded, breaking into a smile that lit up his entire face. "Good."

A group of four women sat down at the other table, their conversation and laughter very loud.

Alannah and Connor ate in silence for a couple of minutes.

"I like your new look," he said. "I like that you're wearing your hair down now, and the color makes you stand out."

"Thank you," she said.

They ate in quiet for a while again, listening to the noises of the street and the rambunctious conversation at the other table.

"So…you don't have a boyfriend?"

She looked across at him. "No."

"What about Trenton Johnson?" He twirled a fry in ketchup. "I've seen him at DymoGenesis a couple of times. Once in a red Maserati." He sounded in awe of the car.

Alannah remembered that day and all the stares when Trenton pulled up front in a red, limited edition Maserati GranTurismo convertible with the obnoxious vanity plate LOVRMAN. Her car had been at the dealer for routine maintenance, and he'd picked her up from work.

"Trenton's only a friend."

Connor lifted his gaze to hers. "Is he? I've heard—"

"What you've heard is wrong," Alannah said firmly, perhaps a little too harshly. She softened the words with a tentative smile. "People misunderstand and always think there's something going on between us, but there's not. He and I are just friends."

He nodded as if he fully understood the nature of their relationship, but then said in a low, disheartened voice, "He's really rich."

Alannah knew that tone well. It was the sound of a man intimidated by her close relationship with Trenton, whose wealth surpassed anything they could ever achieve in several lifetimes. "Yes, he is. And he dates a lot of women. I'm sure you've seen him in magazines, if you pay attention to that kind of thing."

"Not really, but I know who he is because...well, he's a member of the Johnson family."

The Johnson name carried a lot of clout not only in Seattle, but in the country as a whole. They employed thousands and donated millions annually to various charitable organizations. Their personal lives were often fodder for the gossip blogs and tabloids, though they did their best to squash news stories about them and stay out of the spotlight.

"So if you're not dating Trenton Johnson, and there's no one else..."

"There's no one else," Alannah confirmed. She held her breath, sensing he was about to ask a question.

"Would you like to go out with me?" The smile on his face appeared a little nervous, not quite extending into his eyes to quell the anxiety she saw there.

The new and improved Alannah had been asked on a date! Her makeover was working already.

She had to force herself not to grin too hard. "Yes," she said. He didn't make her breathless the way being around Trenton did, but she was certain that, with time, the butterflies would come.

Connor's smile broadened into a full-on grin. "Super. Next week okay?" He picked up his sandwich, as if he'd suddenly regained his appetite.

"Next week is perfect."

Chapter Four

Alannah needed a whole new wardrobe, but a few new outfits would have to do for now. It was Saturday afternoon, and she was going to do some shopping so she'd have something to wear for her date with Connor next Saturday night.

Too bad her girlfriend, Terri, couldn't accompany her on the shopping trip. One of technicians at the day spa and salon had called in sick, and Terri had picked up the extra shift.

"Alannah, honey, I feel so bad about canceling on you." Her voice came through the car's speakers.

Alannah backed her black Lexus LS out of the garage. The leather interior was the color of parchment paper and the wood grain a dark walnut. She'd never owned a new car in her life, until Trenton presented the extravagant gift for her thirtieth birthday, complete with a red bow on top. Despite her protests, she'd loved the car on sight and relished the new car smell.

"I hate you have to cancel, too. You know I have no fashion sense."

"You'll be fine." Terri laughed. "By the way, make sure you get some nice underwear. Nothing like a lacy set of bras and panties to make you feel sexy, and Connor will appreciate the effort, too."

"Um, this is our first date. There's no way he's seeing my

underwear."

"You never know. It may go really well."

"Not that well, Terri," Alannah said, driving to the Stop sign at the end of her street.

"Fine, whatever. Just make sure you get something cute. And whatever outfits you pick, highlight your best attributes. Big booties are in, so play up your advantage."

Alannah merged into traffic. "I don't know…"

"Remember, this is all about the new and improved Alannah. You don't have to hide behind the baggy shirts and all those long skirts. You're not Amish, are you?"

Alannah giggled. "No, I'm not."

"Okay, then. Let loose. And you might as well look around for a few nice evening dresses, too, for when you have to attend one of those fancy events with your other man."

Alannah rolled her eyes. "Trenton is not my man."

"Honey, he's so damn fine, I don't know how you resist jumping his bones every time you see him."

"We're just friends, Terri. How many times do I have to tell you that?"

"Until I believe it. But anyway, if Connor is as hot as you say, who cares about your hot best friend? Hang on." Terri covered the phone, and Alannah heard the muffled tones of her conversation with someone in the salon. Finally, she came back on the line. "Gotta run, my appointment's here. Have fun and I'll catch up with you later. Smooches!"

"Bye."

Alannah disconnected the Bluetooth call and continued to Westfield Southcenter shopping mall. With a massive food court, clothing stores that catered to a variety of tastes, and a movie theater, the largest shopping center in Washington was often crowded. But upon arrival, she lucked out and cruised into a vacant space when another driver pulled out.

In the parking lot outside Macy's, she looked at the six stores on her list. A trip to Soma was a must today. As Terri pointed out, she needed new undergarments.

Right then, the phone rang. Trenton this time.

"What are you doing?" The sound of wind let her know he was driving.

Alannah cradled the phone between her ear and shoulder, folded the list, and tucked it into her purse. "About to do some shopping. I need new clothes."

"New clothes for what?"

"It's all part of my makeover. I need new going-out clothes. Plus, I have a date." She squirted candy-apple-scented sanitizer in her hands and rubbed them together. The silence on the other end of the line prompted her to hold the phone away from her ear and stare at the LCD screen, wondering if the call had been disconnected. "Hey, are you there?"

"I'm here. You have a date, huh? Who is he?"

Alannah thought for a minute. "Someone at work," she hedged.

"The guy you mentioned the other night?"

"Yes."

"Thought you said he had a girlfriend."

"I was wrong."

Another pause.

"You act as if you don't want to tell me about this guy. You know I'm going to have to check him out."

"Actually, that's what I don't want." Alannah pursed her lips.

"What do you mean? I always check out your guys."

"This one's different."

"How's he different?"

"I really like him."

"So you don't want to find out if he's a good guy or not because you really like him?" When he said it like that, it sounded ridiculous.

"It's not that." Alannah watched the families coming in and out of the mall's entrance. A boy and a girl skipped in front of their parents, and a mother juggled numerous bags while reaching for her son's hand. "I don't want you to scare him off," she admitted.

Trenton chuckled, as if she were being silly. "I won't scare him off."

"You always scare them off, and this time I don't want him to leave."

"If he's a real man, he won't."

"Trenton…" She had to make him see reason. Connor was already intimidated by him, and his big brother routine could spoil the relationship between them before it even started.

"All right, fine. I won't scare him off, but I want to meet him. That's nonnegotiable."

"You will eventually."

Alannah looked down at her hands. They'd been down this road before. Trenton always screened her boyfriends, but she wanted him far away this time. She'd had lunch again with Connor yesterday and could tell he was different. Sweet and honest, he was the kind of man she needed to help her get over Trenton.

She climbed out of the car. "I have to run. I'm about to go into the mall. Sadly, on my own. Terri was supposed to come with me, but she had to cancel because of work. What are you up to today?"

"Nothing. Want some company?"

Alannah closed the door and stood beside the car. Trenton's question made her frown. "Company for what?"

"Shopping."

"*Shopping?*"

"Yes, I'll take Terri's place."

"Huh?"

He laughed, a rich, sexy sound that made her toes curl in her low-heeled sandals. "Seriously. I'll come and give you my opinion—from a male point of view, which is probably better anyway."

"Trent, you hate shopping. If it weren't for your stylist, you'd wear the same clothes every season."

Asking Trenton to go shopping was like inviting a child to the dentist. Neither looked forward to the painful experience.

He never shopped for girlfriends. The task of purchasing their gifts was delegated to his assistant. He never even shopped for himself, employing the same stylist as several Hollywood leading men. She consulted with him on a regular basis about his wardrobe, and when he had a special event to attend, he gave her a call. Every few months she flew up with a barrage of selections. They went through his closet and discarded the old, brought in the new, and when the new season started, they did the same all over again.

"I hate shopping, but I'm not that bad. Besides, I'll make an exception for my buddy."

"Okaaay, if you're willing, I'm fine with you coming to offer your opinion. But I don't want to hear any whining if I take too long."

"I promise not to whine. Where are you?"

"Westfield Southcenter. I'm going into Macy's right now."

"I'm not too far away. I'll meet you at the front door in ten, maybe fifteen minutes."

When Trenton arrived, Alannah's heart leapt. He'd shaved and cut his hair since she last saw him and wore jeans and a black V-neck shirt that played up the color of his swarthy skin and left his tatted arms bare. Even in those ordinary clothes he turned heads.

He stopped in front of her, his grin large, lazy, and sexy. "Ready?"

Taking a breath to still her racing heart, Alannah nodded. "Let's go."

CHAPTER FIVE

Trenton stood behind Alannah on the escalator to the women's department of Macy's.

Her hair was braided into a single thick plait that rested over her right shoulder, and she wore fitted jeans, unusual for her, but without being indecent. Unlike the short-shorts she'd had on the other day, which he still found disturbing.

An oversized shirt drooped off her right shoulder. It was only a shoulder, but he wasn't accustomed to seeing Alannah dressed like that. She usually covered up. Everything. That had to be the reason why his gut tightened when he saw her, and his eyes were drawn to the exposed skin, again and again.

In the women's department, they browsed racks of clothes and accessories. According to what she'd told him, she was on the hunt for a jumpsuit and two dresses—one for a formal occasion and another she could wear out to dinner or somewhere informal.

Minutes into the search, Trenton held up a blue jumpsuit with long sleeves. "What about this?"

A few feet away, Alannah wrinkled her freckled nose. "I want something a little more edgy."

"Edgy?" he echoed, but she'd already moved away.

Trenton continued his search. Glances from women came his

way every now and again with the occasional smile, but he focused on working his way through the racks. A few times he held up an article of clothing for Alannah's approval, and each time she alternated between shaking her head and wrinkling her cute little nose.

After a while, Trenton knew he'd made a mistake. Now he remembered why he avoided clothes shopping, and especially with a woman. This excursion could take forever, and there were other things he'd much rather be doing that were less painful, more interesting, and less time-consuming. Such as watching paint dry or driving nails into his hand with a sledgehammer.

"I'm tired," he announced, and looked up. He searched the area for Alannah but she was across the sales floor, talking to one of the sales reps. He sauntered over to join the conversation.

"That's what I'm here for," the saleswoman was saying. Too much makeup covered her light brown skin, and her almond-shaped eyes slanted upward to give her an exotic appearance. She glanced in his direction when he walked over, and her expression changed to one he'd grown accustomed to since his teen years—one of female appreciation. "May I help you?"

"This is my friend," Alannah said. "He's helping me pick out my outfits."

"Well, it's always nice to have a male perspective." She looked him up and down, unmistakable interest flashing in her eyes, before she returned her attention to Alannah. "Here's what we'll do. I'll pull together some outfits based on what you told me you'd like. I already have the perfect idea for a dress. With your red undertones, it would look beautiful. Adding the right amount of color to your cheeks, with a smoky eye, would bring the outfit together." Excited at the prospect of dressing Alannah, the inflection of her voice surged higher and she talked with her hands. "We'll have sort of a runway experience where you try on the different outfits with the accessories. And your friend"—she cast another lustful look at Trenton—"can help you decide. Sound good?"

"Sounds like a plan to me." Alannah looked up at Trenton. "You okay with that?"

"As long as I don't have to walk around anymore, I'm fine. I'll gladly be a judge."

"The fitting room is over there," the saleswoman said. She touched a hand to the name tag on her chest. "I'm Julia."

"Alannah."

"Trenton."

"Alannah, Trenton, there are seats near the fitting rooms where you can sit down. Give me a few minutes and I promise you won't regret it."

"Thank you." Julia walked away and Alannah clapped her hands together rapidly. "I'm so excited. Wish I'd done this before."

Trenton flung an arm around her shoulders. "Come on."

They strode toward the fitting rooms and found a trio of dark blue sofas. They dropped onto the one in the middle, sitting close to each other.

"This should be fun," Trenton said dryly.

"You said you didn't mind," Alannah reminded him.

"I don't mind at all, actually."

Her face screwed up into a doubtful expression.

"Trust me, I'm glad to be seated. This is way more comfortable than running around the sales floor hunting for clothes."

"What did I tell you about whining?"

"I'm not whining."

"You are. Not everyone can afford to have a stylist shop for them, pick their clothes, and drop them off with the snap of a finger."

"You don't know what you're missing." Trenton slumped in the chair and spread his legs so that his knee bumped Alannah's. Crossing his arms, he let his head fall to the back of the sofa and closed his eyes. "Wake me when she has your outfits picked out."

"Don't fall asleep." Alannah nudged him with her elbow.

He kept his eyes closed. "Quit."

Alannah rested her head on his left shoulder—a comfortable, familiar position. "Julia is a personal shopper for the store. Why didn't I think of this before?"

The scent of honeysuckle filled his nostrils, and Trenton turned his face into her hair. This time he didn't just enjoy the smell. He reveled in it, and a curious sensation rippled across his abs.

He tugged her braid to distract from the feeling. "You told me not to fall asleep, and look at you. Don't *you* fall asleep."

"I won't." She giggled, settling more snugly against him. As if she belonged there. But she did belong, and could always have his shoulder to lean on.

"Don't be too sure. I've been told plenty of times I have a very comfortable shoulder." He didn't know why he said that. Almost as if he had to, because something felt off.

She didn't respond at first, but then she whispered, "I bet." Her voice sounded odd when she said that.

He sat up.

"What do you think?" Alannah grinned from ear to ear. Examining her image in the mirrors, she turned this way and that.

"Where's the rest of it?" Trenton asked.

Julia laughed. "This is the whole dress." She smoothed the material over his friend's left hip.

Alannah tilted her head at her reflection. "Do you have a smaller size? This is a little big up top."

Julia shook her head. "You don't need a smaller size." She pulled the edges at the back so the bodice flattened against Alannah's body and emphasized her small bust to a distracting level. "Maybe a little tailoring at the top, but the skirt fits you perfectly. You've got some hips, so we don't want to go too small."

"What do you think, Trent?"

They both looked at him expectantly, eyebrows raised, waiting for an answer. His throat tightened and he willed his eyes not to lower to her breasts.

"Looks a'ight," he replied.

Alannah pursed her lips and turned sideways to the right, showing off the length of one creamy leg to mid-thigh. Then she shifted to the left. His eyes narrowed on the freckles spattered across her back. For anyone to see. Definitely showing too much damn flesh. Practically naked.

A vein in his temple throbbed.

"I like it, but let's try something else. This is definitely a possibility." Alannah shot him the thumbs-up sign before hurrying back to the dressing room.

Trenton let out the breath he'd been holding and swiped a hand down his face, removing the small beads of sweat that had popped out. What the hell kind of outfits had Julia picked? Alannah was a nice girl, not one of those women who showed all their goods for the world to see.

Before too long, both women returned. This time Alannah wore a short black dress that, in his opinion, barely covered her ass and hugged it too much.

"What the hell is that?" Heart racing, he shot to his feet. "Half the dress is missing."

That dress was unacceptable. *Un-ac-ceptable.*

Two sets of eyes widened in surprise and looked at him.

"It's a cocktail dress," Julia answered.

"I see that. A real *cock*tail dress." Heat prickled the nape of his neck and he swallowed the tightness in his throat.

Alannah sent a strange look in his direction.

Julia frowned at him. Black, high-heeled sandals dangled from her fingers, and sparkly things like jewels covered the thin straps. To his dismay, she bent down and encouraged his friend to put on what could only be classified as hooker pumps.

Alannah slipped them onto her feet, and a transformation took place. The heels had her calves looking right, and her posture improved. Overall she looked fantastic. Taller and sexy, with elongated legs and her butt displayed in all its round, grabbable glory in a dress that left *absolutely* nothing to the imagination. Trenton's stomach knotted up, and his blood pressure spiked high enough to cause heart failure.

Alannah took two steps in the heels and twisted her ankle. He almost ran to her, but Julia was there, lending a steady hand.

"Careful," Julia said. "You can't walk like you're in tennis shoes. You have to move those hips, and you have plenty."

Staring down at her feet, Alannah let out a low-pitched, nervous laugh. "I guess I'll have to practice. I've never worn heels this high." Chewing the corner of her mouth, she shot a look in Trenton's direction. "What do you think?" she asked timidly.

"I don't like it," he answered, shaking his head vehemently.

Julia gawked at him. "What's not to like? She's got great legs, and now they're shown off in a nice pair of shoes. The dress fits her body perfectly—emphasizing her best attributes in a positive way. It's all about finding clothes appropriate for your body type."

Trenton scowled. "Who asked you?"

Alannah gasped. "Trent!"

He pointed at her. "Stay right there. Don't move."

He marched onto the sales floor and moved swiftly through the racks, spotting and pulling two dresses much more appropriate for Alannah to wear. Then he hurried back to both women—Alannah shooting Julia an apologetic smile and Julia standing with her hands linked together in front of her and her mouth set in a flat line.

Clutching a dress in each hand, Trenton held them up like trophies. "These are better." Both were long-sleeved. The black dress would probably fall right below the knee, and the multicolored dress should reach her around the ankles. He held the black one toward Alannah. "And this one has sparkly things on it and it's black, so it's perfect as an evening dress or cocktail dress or whatever."

Alannah and the salesperson looked at each other. He chose not to decipher the look. Alannah trusted him and had trusted him and his opinion for over twenty years. His opinion held much more weight than some saleswoman looking to pimp her out like a common prostitute.

A tight, close-lipped smile lifted the corners of Alannah's mouth. "Would you excuse us for a minute?" Julia nodded and went to straighten sweaters at a table out of earshot.

Folding her arms, Alannah shot Trenton what she thought was her angry stare, where she furrowed her brow and pursed her lips. Instead, she looked absolutely adorable, but now wasn't the time to mention it. He was upset and she was annoyed.

"I know what you're doing, and you don't have to do this. Really," she said.

"Really? Cause I'm worried you're going to catch a cold in those dresses."

Alannah raised an eyebrow at him but he kept his expression blank.

She sighed and rolled her eyes to the ceiling. "You're doing what you always do, the big brother routine. I get it, I'm showing a lot of skin."

"So then what are you doing? You look indecent!" He sounded like a ninety-five-year-old man. But he couldn't think of anything else to say.

Her eyes stretched so wide he could clearly see the muted green ring around the brown. "Are you serious?"

"Yes, I'm serious. You look like a damn prostitute."

Her face flushed red, and that's when he realized he'd gone too far. A dull ache of regret filled his chest.

"You should go," she said in a tight voice. She spun around and wobbled toward the dressing room.

Trenton tossed the dresses on the sofa. "Wait." He rushed around in front of her—easy to do, since she couldn't move very fast in the heels. "I didn't mean what I said—"

"You said I look indecent. You said I look like a prostitute."

"Maybe I shouldn't have said that." Trenton rubbed his forehead, in search of a better way to express the turbulent emotions he'd felt when he saw her transformation. "It's just…you don't have to do all of…this." He waved a hand at the entire disturbing ensemble.

A customer smiled at them and sidled by into one of the dressing rooms.

"You date women who look like *this* all the time, Trent," Alannah said in a low, brittle voice. She folded her arms.

"That's different."

"How is it different? Because it's me? How else am I going to get noticed if I don't look like everyone else?"

"What do you want to be noticed for?" he demanded.

She shook her head and spoke in a low, controlled voice. "You don't get it, do you? Of course not, because people like being around you. You walk into a room and everybody, women *and* men, flock to you. Women throw themselves at you *every single day,* I mean"—she lowered her voice and darted a gaze in Julia's direction—"she would have jumped you if I hadn't been standing right there. You don't understand what it's like for the rest of us. To be invisible."

It never occurred to Trenton that Alannah thought of herself in that way. She dated and had plenty of friends. "You're not invisible."

"Yes, I am."

"No, you're not," he insisted. He had to rid her of that ridiculous notion.

"Most of my friends are your friends. The only time anyone notices me is when I'm with you."

Trenton edged toward her, anger pulsating through his muscles. He couldn't stand to hear her talk about herself in such a negative way. "You're wrong. Your perception—"

"My perception is my reality."

Had she always felt this way? He wanted to fix this but didn't know how. "You don't have to do this, though. You're fine the way you are."

"It's not enough. I want to be lusted after and checked out and whistled at like other women." Staring at her feet, Alannah restlessly plucked the hem of the dress.

Trenton grasped her wrists. He ducked his head and stared into her eyes. "You're better than other women. The kind of attention you're going to get is from men like me—men who only want to use you. You don't want that kind of attention, do you?"

Sadness shimmered in the depths of her eyes. It killed him to think that he was the reason her earlier euphoria had been dampened, but he had to get through to her.

"Just once, I don't want to be the good girl, or the nice one. Just once, *I* want to be the pretty one. In my college yearbook, someone wrote I'd make a nice wife one day. Who writes that? I want men to look at me and want to…screw my brains out."

Trenton dropped her hands and took a step back, from shock as well as the lurid thoughts that immediately came to mind. *Unacceptable* for him to think about his best friend in this way.

Naked. Legs in the air. Getting screwed. *By him.*

He suddenly became aware of his heart's rigorous pounding against his thoracic cavity.

"Do you know what I mean?" Her eyes pleaded for understanding.

A tightness lodged in his chest and Trenton struggled for air, harsh breaths banging the walls of his lungs like bumper cars threatening to bounce off track. "Yeah, I know what you mean."

Unfortunately.

CHAPTER SIX

Alannah bought the first dress and left the other outfits behind. She and Trenton exited Macy's in quiet, an unusual occurrence for the two of them.

"I'm done for the day," she announced. They stopped in front of the main entrance to the mall. Her excitement about the shopping trip had dulled dramatically. She'd made a mistake accepting Trenton's offer of help.

Trenton didn't argue, but his wrinkled brow conveyed his contrition. "About what I said, Lana…I'm not used to seeing you like that, and it threw me, that's all."

"I understand. I have to get used to the changes, too, but I'm excited."

"Obviously." He scratched his head and scanned the busy mall.

"There's nothing wrong with change," Alannah pointed out.

"There's good change and bad change. Once you start dressing a certain way, men start looking at you and thinking things. It's not right. You're…special." He swallowed.

Translation: boring, plain. Invisible.

"I'm not walking down the street half naked. The clothes fully cover me."

"I know, I know. Still…" He frowned. "This guy you're trying to impress—if he can't see you for who you are right now, then maybe he doesn't deserve you. He might not be right for you."

"I'm making these changes for me, not him."

"I don't want you to make a mistake."

"And you haven't made mistakes? I've warned you about certain women, but you don't listen. Remember when you wanted to impress that woman who makes the energy bars? You actually tried to adopt a vegan diet."

"Don't remind me," he groaned. He covered his face with a hand. "Worst forty-eight hours of my life."

Alannah grinned. "I told you something about her rubbed me the wrong way." Truth be told, all of his entanglements rubbed her the wrong way. Some more than others.

That particular woman turned out to have a very specific agenda. She hadn't been interested in Trenton, but went out with him because their high-profile relationship brought much needed publicity to her company.

"I remember, I remember."

"And let's not forget the one with the ridiculously huge breast implants."

"Who?"

"Don't act like you don't know who I'm talking about. The one who wanted to land a Playboy spread. What was her name? Boobies McBoobage, wasn't it?"

He chuckled, almost doubling over with laughter. "Come on now, she wasn't that bad."

Alannah quirked an eyebrow at him. "Oh, really? She looked ready to tip over. Didn't she wear a back brace so she wouldn't?"

"Now you're just being mean."

Alannah shrugged. "All I'm saying is, we're both adults, and we're going to make mistakes. But even with that, I don't think this guy is a mistake."

He watched her in silence for a moment, and then flipped his gaze to the shoppers milling around. "I wish you would at least let me know who he is." He brought his eyes back to her.

"I will in time."

"You keep this up, and I'm going to start thinking he's an ex-con." Trenton sighed. "But I'll leave you alone for now. Come here."

"I'm not hugging you."

"Come in for the hug." He motioned with his hands. "You know you have to get the hug."

She groaned, pretending to be upset, but when he pulled her into his arms and kissed the top of her head, she felt as if she were right where she should be and didn't want to let go. Her cheek rested against his firm chest, and she inhaled his Trenton smell. He didn't have on cologne today, so it was just him—pure masculinity and achingly familiar. She squeezed her eyes shut and hugged him tight, wishing…wishing he would see her as more than someone he had to protect.

When she felt as if she would drown in her emotions, she pulled back. "Okay, that's enough." She bit her bottom lip to keep it from trembling.

Trenton took a couple of steps back and cleared his throat. "I better go," he muttered, almost to himself.

They said their goodbyes and he sauntered away. Alannah watched his progress down the wide hallway to the exit. He moved slow and easy, with long, confident strides. The black shirt hugging his broad back, and a full head above almost everyone he passed.

At the doors he turned, waved to her, and walked out into the sun.

****

On Sunday, Alannah met Terri for brunch at a French bakery on Queen Anne Avenue. The big red house served as a gathering spot for residents of the neighborhood and offered an assortment of sweet and savory pastries in addition to breakfast and lunch.

She settled into a chair on the front porch and idly perused the menu, although she knew it by heart. She needed to kill time since Terri was late, as usual. Right as she decided to have the croque monsieur, Terri bounded up the stairs and sashayed over in a pair of tight, worn jeans.

Terri had the kind of shape that made anything remotely fitted look indecent, but had no qualms about showing off her body. She owned her figure, and Alannah envied her I-don't-give-a-crap attitude.

Blond braids hung over one shoulder, and as she walked, her ample hips caught the attention of the male half of a couple exiting the restaurant. The man turned his head to stare at her butt and was popped in the back of the head by his female companion. Terri missed the entire episode unfolding, but Alannah was used to seeing men react to her in that way.

Terri spread her arms wide. "Hey, honey, how are you?"

Alannah stood and gave her a warm hug.

Terri grinned. "I love the hair. The color turned out fabulous."

Alannah blushed. "Thanks." The stylist in Arizona had used the specific color Terri had recommended.

"How was your trip?" Her friend settled into a chair and picked up the menu.

"It was nice to get away and see my parents again." Alannah gave Terri a quick rundown of her activities while on vacation and then set a snow globe on the table. "Voilà. I brought this back for you." The souvenir had *Arizona* across the bottom and inside a cactus and a man on a horse.

Terri's eyes lit up with delight. "You didn't have to bring me back anything." She snatched up the souvenir and caressed it the way a fortune-teller rubbed a crystal ball.

"Now you can add it to your collection."

"Thank you." She slipped it into her purse and then crossed her arms on the table. "You know, you never told me what Trenton thinks about the new you."

Before Alannah could go into details, the waitress arrived and they placed their orders.

Afterward, Terri set her chin in her hand, her expectant expression making Trenton's lackluster response even more embarrassing to share.

Alannah schooled her features into an expressionless mask, even though heavily disappointed. "His reaction was pretty nonexistent. He doesn't really care one way or the other how I look."

"He didn't say anything at all?"

"Only that the changes were 'nice' and 'different.' Whatever that means."

"Oh."

"He doesn't care, Terri. Stop trying to be a matchmaker. We're friends. That's it."

A car passed by slowly. The driver cast his eyes back and forth, looking for parking on the crowded street.

"So what's next?" Terri asked.

"I'm going to continue my summer makeover. I feel so much better about myself because of the changes."

Terri folded her arms on the table. "How can I help?"

"Going shopping with me will help. Trenton met me at the mall yesterday and it was a total bust."

"What happened?"

Alannah gave her a quick summary of their short trip to Macy's.

"Yikes," Terri said, frowning. "You two have the strangest relationship, but don't worry, mama's here." She patted Alannah's hand. "What exactly are you looking for?"

"In general, new clothes. I found a few outfits in Arizona when my sisters dragged me to the mall, but I need more. Clothes that are nothing like the frumpy crap I'm always wearing. I want to show off my figure. What little figure I do have."

"You have a great figure."

"I have no boobs. You, on the other hand…" She stared with envy at Terri's ample chest.

Her friend waved away the remark. "Honey, these things are a blessing and a curse, believe me."

"More of a blessing," Alannah muttered, noting the way Terri's cleavage peeked out the top of her neckline.

"Tell you what, you can have my breasts and I'll take Trenton as my best friend, because friendship has its privileges." She looked pointedly at Alannah's car parked across the street.

Heat filled Alannah's cheeks. "I didn't ask for it."

"But you love it, don't you?"

"I thought it was too much when he gave it to me."

"Yet you didn't turn it down?"

"How could I? Once I drove it, I couldn't say no. The leather is so comfy and plush, there's a start/stop button, massaging seats..." She sighed. She could never have afforded such an expensive vehicle with all the options Trenton had tossed in. To give her peace of mind, he'd even covered maintenance and repairs on the car.

"And then there's that." Terri pointed to the one-of-a-kind Marc Jacobs bag on the chair. Made of soft calf leather, the cashew-colored purse had Alannah's initials—AB—as a buckle in solid gold on the front. Trenton knew the designer personally and had requested he create something special for her last Christmas. The bag had no retail value. It was literally priceless, because there wasn't another one like it in the world.

"Not to mention all the trips you've taken with him and his family. He takes care of you the way a man takes care of his wife. You guys are practically a couple already, you just don't have the sexual component. So yeah, I'd gladly take him off your hands. There aren't too many men doing favors like he does without expecting something in return." Terri arched a threaded brow.

That was the problem. He spoiled her. No doubt about it. He was very generous, and she had all the benefits of a relationship—without the relationship.

Alannah swallowed the tennis-ball-sized lump in her throat.

She'd like to cut herself off from him completely, go cold turkey, but that would be the equivalent of getting off a highly addictive drug like meth or heroin. The results could be disastrous.

"So when do you want to go shopping again?" Terri asked, recapturing her attention.

"You free next Saturday?"

"Yep."

"Perfect." Alannah felt her spirits lifting already. She held up her glass of water. "To new beginnings."

"To new beginnings, and bringing out your inner wild child." Terri growled low in her throat and tapped her glass against Alannah's.

Alannah laughed and swallowed a mouthful of water. With her friend's encouragement, she felt confident she'd be successful with the planned changes. This summer a brand new Alannah would emerge. And if all went well, she'd be able to leave her feelings for Trenton Johnson far behind.

Chapter Seven

Alannah had told Trenton to use his key when he came over for dinner. He entered the townhouse and paused when he heard a low growl. The sound came from the wall near the staircase, in the small cage holding her Yorkie, Angel. He had no idea why the dog hated him so much.

She either barked at him like he was an intruder, or scampered into the cage to avoid him altogether. Once she'd even used her paw to pull the door shut. Then she'd plopped down on the pillow with her back to him, as if she couldn't stand the sight of him.

"What the heck is wrong with that damn dog?" he'd asked Alannah once. "Everybody likes Trenton."

"Probably because you talk about yourself in the third person." Angel had growled at him from Alannah's arms.

"That has nothing to do with it. She's just a bitch. Literally."

Alannah had frowned. "Did you do something to her?"

"No, but I should. Hate that damn dog."

"Stop." She'd covered the dog's ears and held her closer. "She'll hear you. And stop calling her 'that damn dog.' She's sensitive. Her name is Angel."

"Devil is more like it," he'd said below his breath.

"What did you say?"

"Nothing."

Right now, Angel stood on the padded floor of the cage on four stubby legs, body taut, tail straight up in the air, and lancing Trenton with the meanest face she could.

"I regret the day I bought you, you know that?" he said in a fierce whisper.

She barked at him and then made another low growl, as if contemplating his demise.

"Angel my ass," Trenton grumbled.

He followed his nose to the kitchen, from where he smelled an enticing scent, which meant Alannah was hard at work. For years he'd been her guinea pig when she tried new recipes. He couldn't wait to taste the new creation.

When he entered the kitchen, he heard Boa's "Eat You Up" on low, coming through the iPod speakers sitting on a corner of the breakfast bar. Alannah smiled when she saw him, and his heart did an odd little flip that stopped him in his tracks.

Where did that come from?

He rubbed his chest to alleviate the odd sensation. "Almost done?"

"Almost. Get ready for a masterpiece," she boasted.

She turned back to the stove, which gave him a chance to take a good look at her. Her auburn tresses were pulled up into a high ponytail, and she wore a thin black T-shirt that looked like it was at least one size too small. Something the old Alannah would have never done. He did, however, recognize the oversized sweatpants.

She started dancing to the music. "This is going to be so good," she sang.

"Please stop," Trenton said. "You're the most uncoordinated black woman—no, black person—I know. The only reason you still have your black card is because I bribed a bunch of folks during the appeal process so you could keep it."

"You're just jealous of my moves. Bet you can't do this." Alannah performed a very awkward moonwalk.

"Michael Jackson is rolling over in his grave right now." He shook his head. "Sorry, Michael. I tried to stop her."

She stuck out her tongue and returned her attention to the stove.

Trenton took a seat in one of the high-backed wood barstools at the breakfast bar, in front of a tall glass of lemonade, and watched her work. He licked his lips, mouth watering from the scent of the rib-eye steak.

On occasion a personal chef cooked his meals whenever he wanted to eat at home and didn't feel like cooking himself, and he also had the option of going to his mother's house and eating some fine cooking from Adelina. Yet there was something about Alannah's food that always tasted that much better and brought him comfort.

She was much better than she used to be. He recalled her failed attempt at making bananas foster.

"What are you smiling about?" she asked. She set a rib eye on a plate in front of him and spooned blue cheese sauce over it. His stomach danced in anticipation.

"Thinking about the time you almost burned down the kitchen trying to make bananas foster."

She swirled the sauce around the plate. "What a mess. I can't believe the towel caught fire like that."

Trenton chuckled. "Be glad it wasn't worse."

She joined him in the laughter, but kept her eyes on the plate, concentrating on the artistry of the dish. "I am glad, believe me."

"Even with that mess and the panic, the bananas turned out delicious," he pointed out.

"They did, didn't they? I should try that recipe again. I've been too nervous to attempt it because of the near accident."

"I'm sure your flambé skills will be much better now."

Alannah spooned roasted potatoes beside the steak. "Then, of course, there was The Great Quiche Incident of '09."

Trenton groaned.

"I can't believe you ate so much of it and didn't say anything." Alannah shook her head in disbelief. "I gagged once I tasted it myself."

"I didn't want to hurt your feelings, but man, that was some nasty stuff."

"You really took one for the team, and I appreciate it. Thank goodness for The Best Thai Restaurant." She spooned creamed spinach beside the steak and used a paper napkin to swipe the circumference of the plate for a cleaner look. She finished by dropping chopped parsley onto the potatoes as a garnish.

"Oh yeah, that was the first time we ate there." With dinner a bust, they'd driven to the restaurant to get something to eat and had been loyal customers ever since.

Alannah cut into the steak. She twisted it in the blue cheese sauce and then blew on it. "Tell me what you think of this." She lifted the fork to his mouth.

Trenton leaned in, pulled off the meat, and chewed. Well seasoned and cooked to a perfect medium rare. Delicious. "Mmm…that's good."

She pumped a fist. "Yes! You really like it?"

"Mhmm." He yanked away the fork and knife. She giggled as he cut another piece of meat. "I can't believe how good this is." The creamed spinach and roasted potatoes tasted perfect, as well. He could have been dining in a fine restaurant. "This is better than your steak and mushroom gravy."

"No way. You love that dish. You rave about it for days every time I make it."

"I know, you don't make it enough," Trenton said around a mouthful of food, enjoying the dish too much to stop eating long enough not to talk with his mouth full. He pointed at the plate with the fork. "But seriously, I'm saying this is even better, so you know it's good."

"Great," Alannah said with satisfaction. She skipped back to the stove. "This is good practice, because I'm serving it to my new guy friend for dinner on Friday night."

A piece of meat lodged in Trenton's throat. With difficulty, he swallowed it and then took a big gulp of lemonade. He cleared his throat. "You're cooking for him now?"

She and the mystery man had only been going out for a few weeks.

Alannah piled dirty dishes into the sink. "I like him," she said. As if that made it okay.

"You're doing a lot for this guy and I haven't met him yet." He tried to keep the edge out of his voice, but this character was now encroaching onto sacred turf. She hardly ever cooked for anyone else except Trenton, and when she did, it was usually family or close girlfriends.

"And you're not going to meet him."

"Excuse me?" He must have misunderstood her.

"I *said*, you're not going to meet him."

"Why not?" Trenton demanded. He set down the knife and fork.

Alannah turned to face him and placed her hands on the edge of the counter behind her. "I don't mean you'll never *ever* meet him, but you won't right now. I really like this guy and you know how you get—all big brother-ish on me."

"Because I care about you. I have to weed out the bad ones. Is that a crime?"

"Trust me, he's a good one." A beatific smile filled her face, and his heart sank with the force and velocity of an anchor in the sea. Was she really that much into this guy?

"If he's a good one, let me meet him," he said.

"*No.* You'll intimidate him. He already knows we're best friends, and he's still interested. Most men can't handle when they find out I'm best friends with someone as stinking rich as you are."

He gritted his teeth. "Whose fault is that? A real man wouldn't fall back because the woman he's interested in has a rich best friend."

She tilted her head at him. "You know good and well that's not true. You men have very fragile egos, and I don't want him to run off before we've even had a chance to really get to know each other."

Having lost his appetite, Trenton tossed his napkin onto the counter. "Do you know how ridiculous you sound? It's as if you'd rather find out later that he's a jerk than finding out now. That's why I have to screen these guys. I'm a man and I know what to look for."

She sighed dramatically. "You're a man, and you chase them off. Between your money and your good looks and the fact that you can become *very* overbearing, it's a wonder I've been able to keep boyfriends over the years. And really, they've only been the ones that you approved of. All the others have run off."

"Because they're scared punks," he bit out.

"Because you scare them off," she corrected.

Trenton tapped his forefinger on the top of the bar. "At least tell me this Negro's name."

Something flitted across her features that he couldn't decipher, and she bit the inside of her lip.

"What's that look?"

"If I tell you his name you'll end up doing a background check, and I don't want any negativity about him. I *really* like him, Trent."

"Again, you sound ridiculous. As if you'd rather find out the bad things *after* you've already fallen for him. Can you at least tell me his first name? That won't hurt, will it? That way I can stop calling him 'that guy.'" All he needed was a first name. He already knew the competition—er, rather, the other guy—worked at her job. He could easily figure out the rest.

An odd expression came over face again, as if she was hiding something. "His name is...Connor."

"Connor?" Trenton frowned. Then he guessed why she'd reacted so oddly when he initially asked for a name. "Wait a minute, is he black?"

"There are black men named Connor," she said. Her eyes briefly darted away from his.

"But is *he* black?" he pressed.

"No, he's white," she said, and folded her arms defensively across her chest.

"*He's white?*"

"So what?" she asked defiantly.

"You're dating white men now?"

"You've dated white women, or slept with them"—she waved a hand dismissively—"or whatever you do with women."

He ignored her snide remark. "I have dated white women, but..."

She placed a hand on her hip. "But what?"

His mouth clamped shut. He couldn't think of a valid argument against her dating interracially, but he couldn't hold his annoyance in, either. "You're all over the damn place."

"Your ridiculous hypocrisy is showing," she said.

Trenton rubbed his forehead. He was getting a headache. "I don't understand what you're doing."

"I'm dating. I'm casting a wider net. It's really not that unusual."

No, it wasn't unusual, but that didn't mean he had to like it.

"I barely even know you anymore," he muttered. She was dating white men, cooking for them, and refusing to let him meet them. A wave of anger crashed through him. Why change the dynamics of their relationship? They had a good thing going here. He jabbed a finger at her. "You know what, you're changing. Ever since you got your hair done and started working on a new wardrobe, you been acting brand new."

The corners of her mouth tightened. "So you don't like anything about my makeover?"

"No, because you're changing, and not in a good way."

Her eyes widened and she didn't respond at first. His accusation seemed to have surprised her. "I'm still the same person. You're the one acting different."

"If I'm acting different, I'm feeding off of the energy you put out." It was always the two of them against the world. "I've always been there for you. I take care of you. I protect you," he said, grasping at straws.

Their gazes locked, and tension bridged the short distance that separated them.

"Maybe I don't need you to protect me anymore."

The quietly spoken words squeezed the air from his lungs. Trenton rested his forearms on the counter and stared down at the plate of forgotten food. "That's what I do." He'd been doing it for years, from the day they met.

Her slippered feet moved quietly on the kitchen floor, and then she stood behind him.

"That's not what I need from you anymore," she said thickly. Her voice reflected what he felt. Emotions bubbling inside of him. A cosmic shift was taking place in their relationship, and he couldn't stop it. His stomach burned from the unnatural fear that overcame him.

Alannah wrapped her arms around his torso from behind and rested her head on his shoulder. "I feel like this is a stupid argument, like you're picking a fight with me. If you're worried about me replacing you, don't be. We've known each other too long and been through too much together. You know me better than anyone else. I'll always need you, Trent, just not in the way I have in the past."

Her words were meant to make him feel better, but they were ugly. And they hurt. They gutted him.

"Things are different now. I'm different, but you're irreplaceable in my life. You're my best friend, Trent. I don't want to lose you…I can't."

The sensation of her heart beating into the muscles of his back provided a bit of comfort, and the sweetness of her scent surrounding him eased his unrest.

Trenton swallowed the lump in his throat, angry at himself for the irrational hurt and anxiety he felt. He had no idea where it stemmed from.

He twisted in the chair and pulled her around so he could cup her face in his hands. He saw the sadness in her hazel eyes and hated being the cause, ashamed of the guilt he'd heaped on her.

Then, as if his vision cleared, he didn't see only a friend he wanted to hug and console. He saw the woman this Connor character undoubtedly saw—skin the color of a milky tea, freckles, and coral-tinted, rosebud lips that invited a man to kiss. The thought that this guy, who placed a smile of bliss on her face so unlike any he'd seen before, would have the pleasure, sent a heaviness into his abdomen.

"You won't lose me," Trenton promised. For now, he wanted to reassure her and wipe the worry from her brow. "I'll always be here." He pulled her into a hug. More for him than for her. He held on tight, her soft body molding into the harder planes of his.

He'd said the right words, but deep down, he knew it was the beginning of the end, and his stomach tangled up into knots. Foreign knots. Knots he'd never experienced before.

She would never lose him. But he knew without a doubt…that he was losing her.

CHAPTER EIGHT

Trenton set down his pen and rubbed his eyes. He hadn't taken a break since he arrived at work this morning, and it was now time for lunch. He was so hungry he felt as if his stomach had turned on itself.

As the senior vice president of sales and marketing, Trenton's office was located on the executive floor of the Johnson Enterprises building, the seat of his family's multibillion-dollar beer and restaurant empire. Decorated with dark wood and leather furniture, the decor and dim lighting had prompted his sister, Ivy, to tease that his office felt more like the VIP room of a club or an exclusive lounge. Exactly the ambience he'd wanted.

When people passed through the door for business, he wanted them to transition into a relaxed state. Doing so put him at a mild advantage and undoubtedly had aided him in negotiating lucrative contracts for the family's lines of beer.

Trenton exited his office and stopped at his executive assistant's desk. Diana, a plus-size sister with a short natural and ass and breasts for days, sat at her computer, reading an email that looked more like a dissertation. No doubt another message from Dave, a sales rep who had lots of ideas for improvements. While Trenton appreciated the suggestions, the young man needed a lesson or two on how to not be so verbose.

"I'm going to lunch with Ivy," he said.

Diana looked up from the screen. "Don't forget your two o'clock staff meeting about the festival."

Johnson Brewing Company, also known as JBC, dispatched reps to the various festivals around the country and the world, but Trenton never missed the Great American Beer Festival, the Oscars for beer makers in the United States.

JBC employed some of the best brewmasters in the industry, so they always brought home awards, but last year they'd won a silver medal in the specialty beer category, where the smaller craft breweries dominated. Having a commercial outfit of their size take home second place had been an unheard of accomplishment. This year they wanted a gold medallion to place on the wall.

"I thought we pushed the meeting back," Trenton said.

Diana shook her head. "We couldn't because the conference call with the Chinese reps was moved up to coordinate with the translators' schedules."

"Oh yeah." Trenton checked his watch. He and Ivy would barely have an hour for lunch, which meant they shouldn't leave the premises. "In that case, would you call downstairs to The Brew Pub and tell them to reserve a booth for me and my sister?" As he walked away, Diana was already picking up the phone to make the arrangements.

Trenton strolled down the hallway to Ivy's office, the executive floor quiet, since half of the staff had already left for lunch. Awards and framed articles about the company's accomplishments in the beer and restaurant industry hung on the walls.

He passed by the empty desk where Ivy's assistant normally sat, knocked twice on the office door, and entered. "Ready to go?"

His "sister" was actually his cousin. Trenton had been brought into the family as a child, after his parents died. From the beginning, his aunt and uncle had treated him as one of their own children, and his cousins had welcomed him as a brother. The fact that his skin was much lighter than their darker tones made others outside the family pause, but had no bearing on their closeness as a family.

Ivy shut her laptop and slowly rolled her neck. "I sure am ready to go. I'm hungry. Starved, actually. Are you?"

"I'm surprised you didn't hear my stomach from my office," Trenton joked. "I have a meeting in less than an hour, though, so we'll have to eat downstairs."

Ivy stepped around the desk in a navy-blue pants suit, her long hair in a sleek bun at her nape. "Fine by me. Today's been a crazy day, so while I'm glad for the break, I have plenty of work to keep me busy when I get back." As the COO of the family's restaurant group, she oversaw the entire operations of their casual dining chain, The Brew Pub, and the high-end restaurants named Ivy's.

Minutes later they'd taken the elevator to the first floor and were nestled in a corner booth of the crowded pub. The chatter of patrons mingled with the clatter of cutlery on plates, and the aroma of hearty burgers, fries, and other pub fare filled the air.

Trenton had a mug of Full Moon beer and a huge steak sandwich in front of him. Ivy had chosen a glass of white wine and a chicken sandwich on a brioche bun. They shared an order of Wreck 'Em fries, the pub's famous appetizer, covered in chili, cheese, and jalapeño peppers. Occasional glances in their direction signaled the building employees and outside customers knew exactly who they were, but no one disturbed them.

"How are the wedding plans coming?" Trenton bit into his sandwich.

His sister had recently become engaged to New York Times Bestselling Author Lucas Baylor, the father of her daughter and a man she'd lost touch with for many years, until they reconnected last year.

"It's coming. Not like this is my first marriage, but Mother wants a huge society wedding, of course."

"Of course." Ivy's first wedding had been a rushed affair without the pomp and circumstance.

"The thing is, Lucas and I haven't picked a date yet, which is a bit problematic when planning something as grand as Mother wants."

"What's the holdup?" Trenton sipped his beer.

"I told Lucas that I didn't want to get married until we found his biological family, and I meant it." Lucas had grown up in the foster care system after being abandoned as a child. "It's the biggest day of our lives, and I want him to have his family there."

"How does he feel about that?" Trenton popped a fry in his mouth.

"He pretends it's not a big deal and says he just wants to get married, but I know it hurts. He wants to know where he's from and he wants to know who he is."

"But hasn't he searched before?"

"He has, but he's never used Cyrus's guy."

At the mention of their older brother, Trenton raised his eyebrows. "Cyrus's guy already ran a background check on Lucas."

"That was a preliminary report to see if there was any dirt on him. I told Cyrus to have him dig deeper, to leave no stone unturned. I don't care how long it takes. I want something for Lucas. Anything."

"If anyone can find Lucas's family, he can. And if you're willing to wait…"

"I'll wait." She smiled tentatively. "I hope I don't have to wait too long, though."

Trenton chuckled. "Too late now. You put it out there."

"I know." She sipped her wine. "Oh, I ran into Lana the other day. Love the changes she's made to her appearance. She looks great, doesn't she?"

Trenton frowned. "Yeah, I guess."

"You guess? She looked fabulous. I almost didn't recognize her." Ivy stabbed the fries with a fork and took a bite. "Her eyes are gorgeous. You can really see them now without the glasses."

Trenton grunted.

Ivy arched a brow. "Okay, what's going on? What am I missing?"

He searched for the right words to articulate his feelings. "She's changing," he said.

"How?"

"She just is."

"I don't understand. Do you not like her new look? I think she looks so much better. Considering the way she used to dress, she made Catholic nuns look like a bunch of hussies."

Trenton chuckled. "Come on now."

"Well…"

"Okay, okay, I get your point, but I know her, and this isn't her. Fixing her hair and getting rid of the glasses aren't so bad, but the way she's starting to dress…I dunno." He shook his head and bit into the sandwich.

"Seriously, Trent, what's wrong with the way she's dressing?"

Trenton finished chewing and swallowed the bite. "What was she wearing when you saw her?"

"Skinny jeans and a really cute top. You have a problem with her clothes? Does she have to run her outfits past you first?" Ivy narrowed her eyes and looked at him with interest.

Trenton took a big bite of his sandwich and chewed slowly, using the time to consider how much of his thoughts to share with his sister.

"I don't think she has to dress the way she's starting to dress to get a man's attention. She's pretty on the inside and out, so it's not necessary. But I have a feeling you're not going to agree with me on the clothes issue, so I'm not even going there. I know you'll agree with me on this, though." He sat forward on the edge of the booth's chair. "She's seeing a new guy, someone from her job. His name is Connor and she says she doesn't want to introduce me to him because I'll scare him off." He snorted. "Ridiculous, right?"

Ivy shrugged. "Doesn't surprise me."

"What?" His hand froze halfway to his mouth with a fry between his fingers.

"You either badmouth the men so bad she breaks up with them, or you scare them off with your big brother routine."

"You're nuts." He waved his hand dismissively and popped the fry in his mouth. "If that were true, why did I encourage her to date TJ in accounting?"

"Because you don't consider him a real threat."

"A real threat to what?"

"Your relationship with Alannah. I swear, sometimes I think you want her to be alone so you can have her to yourself." Ivy paused and narrowed her eyes. "Is *that* it?"

"Of course not. You just accused me of sabotage and what...holding a crush for my best friend? You're being ridiculous." Heat crawled across his scalp.

"I don't think so," Ivy said slowly, eyes narrowing even more. "In fact, now that I think about it, you sabotage all her relationships."

"No, I don't."

"Saboteur," she said, pointing. "How can you even deny it?"

"I let her—"

"You *let* her?"

He sighed and shook his head. "You know what I mean."

"Yes, I'm afraid I do." Ivy wiped her fingers on a napkin and tipped her head to the side. "You don't even see it, do you?"

"See what?"

Her brow wrinkled as she mulled the next words. "You're jealous."

"Are you crazy?" Trenton let out a bark of laughter and dropped his sandwich to the plate. He stared at his sister, who'd clearly lost her mind. "That's my girl, my best friend."

Ivy leaned across the table. "You're jealous, Trent. Admit it," she whispered.

"She's dated guys over the years."

"And they all had to meet your approval."

"So what?" His voice had gotten a little loud, and he stopped right away. He and Ivy glanced around at the other tables, but no one paid attention to them. Nonetheless, he lowered his voice. "I was looking out for her. If you want to know the truth, I was protecting her from men like me. I know the signs and who they are, because I'm that type of guy. She needs someone nice, not a man like me who comes with a lot of baggage. Besides, she's too good for me, and I'd hurt her. If I hurt her, I'd never forgive myself."

Ivy ran her tongue along the inside of her cheek, an odd expression he couldn't decipher on her face. Slowly, he rewound the words he'd spoken.

"Trent," she said gently.

"Don't." His throat tightened and he sat back in the booth. The food on his plate no longer looked appetizing, and the atmosphere at their table took a nosedive.

They stared at each other, and his gut twisted. All of a sudden, the clank of the dishes and conversations at neighboring tables sounded louder.

"You're a good person," she said. "No one is too good for you. You deserve—"

"Stop." He held up a hand and pulled in a difficult breath. He couldn't look at her as he gathered his thoughts. When he lifted his gaze he saw pity in Ivy's eyes, which made him angry. He hated pity. "Stop trying to psychoanalyze me," he said in a hard tone. "You're not qualified."

Ivy nodded. "Okay, I'll stop."

An insufficient response, because she didn't understand. If she did, she wouldn't look at him as if she wanted to pull him into a hug and stroke his head.

"I need to get ready for my meeting," Trenton mumbled. He slipped from the booth.

"Trent."

He pulled out his wallet. They owned the restaurant and didn't pay for meals, but the server had to be tipped. He tossed a hundred-dollar bill on the table.

"Trent," Ivy implored.

He looked into her pleading eyes and flashed a quick, false smile. "I'm fine."

Walking away, Trenton abandoned the meal and his sister's company. Striding through the restaurant, he kept his head held high. He'd call her later and apologize, but right now he had to get out of there and away from the truth he didn't want to face, about himself and his past. The truth of why he'd come to live in Seattle in the first place.

Chapter Nine

"I'm at home now. We're good?" Trenton asked, wrapping up the conversation with Ivy.

He parked his white Range Rover in the garage of his condominium tower on the corner of Virginia and Fourth Avenue, in the heart of Seattle. Only steps to shopping, trendy hotspots, and restaurants, the location offered the convenience of a twenty-four-hour concierge, a rooftop terrace, and a fully equipped gym that he took advantage of whenever he had the opportunity.

"Of course. Take care, okay?" Ivy said.

"I will. Talk to you later."

He disconnected the Bluetooth on the call and pinched the bridge of his nose. He'd called to apologize for his behavior at lunch. They didn't dwell on why he'd reacted the way he did, but she'd accepted his apology.

Trenton exited the vehicle and took the elevator up to his two-bedroom penthouse on the thirty-fourth floor. The cabin opened into a private vestibule and he entered the interior door. After pushing a button on the electronic panel on the wall, the large open space became bathed in light, while at the same time, the low, soothing music of stringed instruments poured through hidden speakers.

He crossed the hardwood floor to the kitchen, a chef's dream that contained a Sub-Zero refrigerator, Miele appliances, and plenty of counter space. It seamlessly flowed into a spacious living room with an eleven-foot ceiling and large windows that spanned the height of the room. During the day he had a clear view of South Lake Union in the distance, but at night the dominant scenery consisted of little squares of lights in the nearby buildings.

Trenton removed a beer from the refrigerator and took a huge swallow, mind still unsettled because the conversation with Ivy made him think about the past. After another swig, he frowned down into the dark brew.

Ivy had accepted his apology because she knew he had some issues. Who wouldn't when your own mother didn't love you enough to keep from hurting you? When she hated you so much she took away the one person she knew you loved most in the world.

He set the beer on the concrete countertop with a heavy hand.

On the way back to his bedroom, Trenton started stripping out of his clothes. The tie he yanked off landed on the bed. The rest of his clothes came off quickly as he tried not to think about his difficult childhood, or why it bothered him so much that Ivy brought it up. Usually he could handle thoughts about his past, but not tonight. He felt off and needed to escape the memories.

Standing naked in the bedroom, he dialed Alannah's number, but the call rang four times and rolled to voicemail. He rubbed the back of his head, where a dull throb had emerged as the memories slithered closer with the dangerous intent of a snake.

"Hey, wanted to see what you were up to tonight. Maybe we can get into something." *Need you.* "Hit me back."

Trenton disconnected the call, knowing she would get in touch as soon as she saw he'd called. In the meantime, he went into the bathroom and entered the glass-enclosed shower stall. He turned on the water as hot as he could stand and lathered his skin, but he couldn't wash away the painful memories of abuse.

He didn't know why his mother didn't love him. At that young age, he had been unable to come up with a reasonable explanation for why she constantly hurt him, and to this day couldn't explain. The therapist had said that the problem lay with his mother, not him. Logically, he understood, but emotionally he grappled with the whys of the situation.

What had he done? What would make her put out cigarettes on his back to "teach him a lesson"? Why did she lock him in a dark closet so often that up until he started college, he could never sleep in total darkness?

Like many abusers, she'd threatened him to prevent him from telling anyone, including his father—because, as she said, not only did he deserve such treatment for his bad behavior, but the consequences would be much worse if the police came to take her away. She'd convinced him his father couldn't care for him because he traveled all the time and he'd be left all alone to fend for himself. A fate, according to her, ten times worse than what he experienced at her hands.

Through snatches of conversation over the years, he'd learned that his mother had been an aspiring dancer, and his birth had killed her chances of going professional. Bitter and angry, she'd turned to drugs, which explained the random rages that usually ended with him suffering in some form or the other—emotional or physical abuse, oftentimes both.

His mother had always been careful to concentrate the attacks on his back and upper arms. Doing so made it easy to hide the damage under his clothes, caused by the cigarettes or the crack of the electric cord tearing through his flesh.

She steered clear of his face, but she'd attacked him there three or four times that he could remember. When she had, it was as if she couldn't help herself. On one occasion she'd given him a black eye, and he'd missed a week of school so she wouldn't have to explain the bruising. Another time she'd hit him across the face so hard, the belt buckle had drawn blood at his temple. To this day he still had a barely visible scar that peeked from behind his hairline. After those episodes, Trenton had learned that keeping his head down was the best defense during her rampages.

He couldn't see the scars on his arms and back anymore and most days didn't think about what they represented—hate, helplessness, to be unwanted, to be unloved. The tattoos hid the marks, but the most important one didn't hide anything. It was on his chest, in the design of a sun. Inside the sun was the anniversary date of his parents' deaths—October sixteenth.

The murder-suicide of his parents occurred when he was seven years old. Neighbors called the police after hearing gunshots in the apartment where he lived with his mother and where his father visited whenever he returned to Philadelphia. The police arrived on the scene to find him covered in blood and initially thought he had been shot. But he hadn't been. The blood belonged to his father.

Within twenty-four hours of learning about the deaths, his Uncle Cyrus, his father's older brother, and his wife Constance flew in, and days later brought him to Seattle amidst the media circus that broke out. During the entire ordeal, the only witness to the crime, Trenton, didn't speak. In fact, he stopped talking for an entire year. Talking had gotten his father killed.

After he told his father what his mother had been doing to him, he came to take him away. Trenton would finally be safe, and they'd be together—except that dream never came true. The day his father came to get him, his mother was in an agitated state. During the resulting argument, where she stood between father and son to keep them apart, his mother produced a gun and shot his father twice, right in front of Trenton.

Then she did the unthinkable. She pointed the gun at her son. He'd closed his eyes, ready to die. Without his father, he no longer had a reason to live. But nothing happened.

Then he opened his eyes. His mother's eyes filled with tears, and whatever demons she'd fought for years finally won. She put the gun in her mouth, pulled the trigger, and blew the back of her head off.

Trenton couldn't remember much else after that. He vaguely remembered crying out—his own voice unrecognizable. He ignored his mother's inert form and flung himself across his father's motionless body. The life-sustaining liquid gushing from his chest covered Trenton's arms and saturated his clothes. He'd never forget that day for as long as he lived.

"Come on, shake it off," Trenton said to himself.

He stepped out of the shower and took a big blue towel off the towel warmer, dried off, and wrapped the towel around his waist. He swallowed two ibuprofen and looked down at his phone. A text from Alannah showed on the screen. He hadn't even heard the message notification, he'd been so distracted by the memories.

At dinner with Connor. Will call you tomorrow.

Trenton stared at the message. No matter what, they always called each other back. He braced his hand on the counter. The headache that beat against his skull exploded and helplessness overwhelmed him.

"Shake it off," he repeated.

He rushed into the bedroom and snatched up his second cell phone, the one he used for the women he dated and other people who weren't family or part of his close circle. He scrolled through the names, selected Beth, and hit Call.

A breathless female voice answered on the first ring. "Trenton?" He could see her now, with a long, silky weave and perfectly made-up face.

"Hey, baby, how are you?" He rubbed his forehead, hoping the pain medicine kicked in soon.

"Fine. I didn't think you'd call."

He forced himself to chuckle. "Why not?"

"I don't know. I haven't heard from you since the last time we hooked up." She sounded uncertain. "But I'm glad you called," she added in a rush.

"I've been busy, but I'm free tonight. How about you?"

"I am. Definitely free."

"Good. Put on your sexiest outfit. I'm coming to get you."

"Where are we going?" she asked, excitement adding even more breathlessness to her voice.

Trenton thought for a moment. He should get away for the weekend and do some partying. "Vegas."

"Oh my gosh, Trenton. Really?" she squealed.

"Really."

"For the night?"

"For the weekend."

"So you already have the tickets?" She sounded skeptical, as if she didn't believe the trip would actually happen.

"We're not flying commercial. We'll use one of my family's smaller planes for the trip down."

"Oh my gosh!" she breathed.

He laughed. Her excitement was contagious.

"What should I pack?"

"Don't worry about all that. Just be sexy when I pick you up. We'll buy everything else you need for the weekend when we get there."

"Ooh, baby, I can't wait to see you. I'm going to do something very, very special for you."

He could only imagine. Beth was a very talented young woman.

"I'll be there in an hour. Make sure you're ready, or I'm leaving without you."

"I'll be ready in thirty minutes!" she promised.

They disconnected the call and Trenton went to the huge, custom-designed walk-in closet. He hit a button on the wall and his wardrobe scrolled by on a metal loop. When he saw the pieces he wanted to wear, he released the button and removed the shirt and slacks.

He sprayed on cologne and dressed in a forest-green shirt that he knew brought out the green in his eyes, and dark slacks. Checking out his reflection in the mirror, he had to admit he looked damn good. Tonight, this weekend, he would enjoy himself and get rid of the negative thoughts.

He smiled at his reflection, rolled his shoulders, popped his neck, and headed out the door.

Chapter Ten

Alannah was staring through a microscope at tissue samples when the loudspeaker in the lab crackled.

"Alannah Bailey, you have a visitor."

She lifted her head, frowning. She wasn't expecting anyone. A few coworkers glanced in her direction. Checking the wall clock, she saw that it was almost lunchtime, a good time to take a break anyway.

She removed her gloves and tossed them in the appropriate receptacle and exited the lab. In the hall, she ran into Connor.

He grinned broadly at her. "Hi there. I had a great time this weekend."

"I did, too," Alannah said. As always, Connor had been a perfect gentleman.

After a rooftop dinner at Hard Rock Cafe, they'd gone down to Pier 57 and taken a ride on the Seattle Great Wheel and used the time in the long line to chat with another couple they'd ended up sharing the gondola ride with. Afterward, the four of them had walked to one of the bars on the waterfront and had drinks.

"You have lunch plans?" Connor asked.

"No, I don't."

"Care to join me? I only have thirty minutes to spare today, so we'll have to eat in the dreaded cafeteria." He shivered.

Alannah laughed at his theatrics, covering her mouth with her hand. "That's fine. I'll suffer through it." She glanced at her watch. "I have a visitor, but I can meet you in say…five minutes or so?"

"Sounds good. I'll see you then."

Smiling to herself, she took the elevator to the first floor. She stepped out of the cab and pulled up short when she saw Trenton leaning on the front desk, chatting up the security guard. Today he wore a black Italian suit, shiny black shoes, and an aqua and green striped tie over a crisp white shirt. Of course, the sight of him made her stomach flutter.

Taking a deep breath, she approached. "Hey."

"Hi there." He grinned, looking as if he was happy to see her.

"What are you doing here?" She stuck her hands in her lab coat.

"I came to eat lunch with you. I thought we could have lunch in the cafeteria."

"You hate eating in the cafeteria."

"Says who? I've never said that."

"Last time you ate here, your exact words were, quote, 'I'm never eating in this nasty-ass cafeteria again,' end quote."

He frowned. "You really need to do something about that sharp memory of yours. It's way too good." He smiled again, in a really good mood. But why wouldn't he be, after the weekend he'd had? "I just want to hang out, that's all."

"I'm not introducing you to him," Alannah said in a low voice, so the guards couldn't hear her.

"What are you talking about? Who? I came to have lunch."

Yeah, right.

Alannah stalked away from the desk to one of the glass walls in the lobby. Trenton followed, and she swung around on him. "I know you. You're not here to have lunch with me. You're here to meet him, but you might as well leave, because I'm not introducing you."

"Why the hell not?" No more smiling.

"Because I'm not. I already explained all of this to you."

"Makes me wonder if there really is a Connor," Trenton said, watching her closely.

"Goodness me, I'm *so* sorry that every time I make a move, my relationship isn't splashed across the magazines and blogs like yours. Looks like you had a fabulous time in Vegas."

She'd promised herself she wouldn't bring it up, but every time she saw him with one of his buxom bimbos, it bugged her. According to the gossip blogs, he and Beth had made quite a splash in Sin City, spending the entire weekend in the most expensive suite at the Wynn hotel. One photo showed Beth standing over his shoulder at a poker game where Trenton had allegedly lost five hundred thousand dollars. But their schedule included more than gambling. They'd partied until almost daylight at one of the clubs at the hotel, and the next day indulged in hours at the spa, getting pedicures and his and her massages. The online article detailed everything they'd done, including the thousands of dollars spent on meals, drinks, and in the clothing stores along the Wynn Esplanade.

"Listen—"

"No, you listen. You don't get to tell me who and when I can date. You obviously don't listen to anything I say. I have no idea what you see in that brainless headcase, but that's your choice. I guess you only like women who giggle and stroke your ego."

"She's not as dumb as she looks," he muttered, sliding his gaze away from hers. At least he had the grace to be embarrassed.

"Yeah, right. Do whatever you want, Trent. I couldn't care less." Alannah crossed her arms.

"If that were true, you wouldn't be so mad."

You have no idea why I'm mad.

"I have to go." She stared across the lobby at the employees and guests filing in and out of the building, but refused to look at him. "Was there anything else?"

"Are you going to look at me?" He stepped close and brought his face to hers, forcing her to look at him. "She's nobody."

Nothing had changed. Nothing would ever change. There were dozens of nobodies in his past, and there would be dozens in the future. Tears welled in her throat, but she held a tight rein on her emotions.

"She likes you a lot, but you're playing games with her feelings. You don't know…" She swallowed and took a shaky breath.

He kept his eyes trained on her. "Fine, I'll leave her alone."

"It's not her, it's just…everything."

She stared down at the speckled tile and bit the inside of her lower lip. She wanted to tell him that it hurt to see him having such a good time with another woman. True, she hadn't been available, but did he have to flaunt his relationships like that?

Neither of them spoke for a long time, and Trenton shoved his hands in his pockets. "You have a good time Friday night?"

"Yes." She didn't look at him. "You have a good time in Vegas?"

"It was okay. I would have preferred hanging out with my favorite girl, but she had plans with another man."

She heard the smile in his voice and lifted her gaze to his. The words pulled at her heartstrings, but she had to stand firm. "I can't be at your beck and call all the time. Whenever you want to do something, I'm just available."

"I see." His eyes grew hard. "Connor takes precedence now, is that it?"

"I didn't say that."

"You didn't have to," he ground out. Rubbing the back of his neck, Trenton glanced out the window. His eyes came back to her. "What is it about this guy that makes him so different from the others?"

"He's a good guy. A really good guy." But that wasn't what was different. *She* was different, because she had to break the hold Trenton had on her heart. "He opens doors and is extremely polite. He has two older brothers, but he's the one who moved back home to help take care of his invalid mother. He hired a nurse for her, but when he leaves work, he goes home and takes care of her, reads to her, and keeps her company in general. When he's not doing that, he does Meals on Wheels, runs marathons for charity, and works with other non-profit organizations."

Trenton frowned. "What is he, a saint?"

"Like I said, a good guy. And he noticed me."

"You get noticed more than you realize." Trenton's voice sounded terse, irritated.

Alannah snorted. "Right."

He kept his eyes on her. "So what about this weekend? You're coming, right?"

This weekend Trenton performed at The Underground, a low-key club with a devoted customer base, owned by one of his frat brothers. Underground hip-hop artists and local bands received good exposure and found ardent fans there. Normally she never missed one of Trenton's performances, but she didn't know if she could stomach it this weekend. Not with the pictures of him and Beth burned into her retina. The women falling all over him at the club would only sicken her more.

"I don't think I can make it."

"Why not?"

"I have plans," she said, unable to think of a lie fast enough.

"Break them."

"I can't."

"You seeing Mr. Perfect again?" A muscle in his jaw tightened.

"Maybe." They hadn't made any formal plans, but she was certain they could find something to get into.

"I'm performing."

"I can't, Trent." Her heart hurt.

"Lana, come on. You never miss our performances." His gaze held hers, eyes angry but pleading at the same time. "You were his last weekend. This weekend you're mine."

The words constricted her heart like tight bands. If he'd let her, every weekend, every single day, she'd be his.

Alannah picked at a thumbnail and let out a breath of resignation, hating herself for being so weak. "Fine, I'll come."

Maybe going out with Trenton wouldn't be so bad, and The Underground was a good place for her to see if the new and improved Alannah could garner more male attention.

Trenton released a relieved breath. "I'll pick you up."

"Sure. The usual time?"

He nodded. "I'll see you Saturday."

"Saturday." Her eyes darted away from his. "I gotta go." She rushed away without looking at him again. Couldn't risk it.

This weekend you're mine.

She blinked rapidly before the tears burning the back of her eyes could fall.

CHAPTER ELEVEN

"I need a favor." Trenton spoke from the doorway of Cyrus's office. His brother, the chief executive officer of the family's beer and restaurant empire, stood in front of the minibar and gulped water, dark skin covered in a thin film of sweat. Every day he came in early to work out in the company gym, and Trenton had stopped in before he became too entrenched in the workday. "I need you to have your guy look into someone for me."

Cyrus drained the bottle and tossed the empty container in the trash. "Who?"

"A guy. All I have is a first name, but I know where he works. He works with Lana, and she's dating him."

Since she and Connor had started dating, the few times she'd talked about him, she'd been starry-eyed and gushed. *Gushed* about him, like he was a rock star. But after his talk with her yesterday, Trenton felt he sounded too good to be true. He allegedly volunteered for all types of organizations, as if anyone had that much time in the week to do volunteer work. From what he could tell, he was patient when it came to sex, too. Trenton was pretty sure they hadn't slept together yet. Connor was either gay or the greatest con artist that ever lived.

He had to find out more about him. Since Alannah refused to

introduce them, he had to take matters into his own hands. No one was that perfect. If he was wrong, then he'd leave well enough alone and let her be happy, and from everything he'd heard about Mr. Perfect, he did what it took to make her happy. Which, ironically, made Trenton sick. So sick his stomach roiled at the thought of them together.

"She's still having you check out her boyfriends?" Cyrus asked.

Trenton came further into the office and rubbed the back of his neck. "Not exactly."

His brother's eyebrow raised in silent question.

"Without going into detail, this is someone I have concerns about, but she doesn't seem to be too worried. But I'm worried, and I want to make sure she's okay and this guy isn't someone who's going to take advantage of her."

"So she doesn't know. Is that what you're saying?"

"Right. It's between me and you."

Cyrus didn't bat an eyelid, the reaction Trenton had hoped for. The one thing he could count on was that his brother would do any and everything to protect the family. Because of her close relationship with them over the years, Alannah was practically family and thus enfolded in the same protective covering.

"What's his name?" Cyrus sat behind his desk. He picked up a pen and pulled a sticky note from the desk draw, which he set exactly perpendicular along the edge of the desk.

"Connor."

"He works at the lab with Alannah?"

"I don't know if he works in the same lab, but he works at DymoGenesis. That much I know. Oh, and he's white."

Cyrus added that notation. "Anything else?"

"That's all I know."

"Okay, I'll get my guy to look into it." If there was any dirt to be found about Connor, his guy would root it out. "What is it about him that's got you concerned?"

Every time he thought about Alannah and her new beau, Trenton became restless. He started pacing. "It's hard to explain. It's not just him, it's her, too. She's changed a lot recently. She's not behaving like the person I've known most of my life."

"That doesn't sound like Lana."

"Trust me, she's not acting like herself. Did you see what she wore to Mother's party the other day?"

Cyrus wrinkled his brow in concentration. "The white—"

"The white and black halter dress with the split up the side." The same dress she'd purchased at Macy's. He'd been hard pressed to quell the urge to cover her with his jacket. "She was walking around without a bra on—like…nah. I didn't like it." The more he spoke, the more agitated he became. "Then she flirted with the Australian from the software company, let him put his hands all over her, like he owned her or something."

"I don't think his hands were all over her—"

"I saw it. Believe me."

"Did he touch her that much?"

"Four times."

Cyrus's brows lifted. "You know the exact number of times."

"Because I watched them. I didn't like that shit one bit. And when I reminded her that she had a man already, you know what she said to me?" He stopped pacing. "She said they weren't exclusive and anyway, she could do whatever she wanted. The Australian's not even her type. She dates men who are quiet and kinda nerdy. That Australian guy was too sneaky and slick-talking, bragging about his business expansion all damn night." The more he talked, the hotter Trenton became. He ran a finger along the inside of his shirt collar.

"I agree he was a little too smooth-talking for my taste, but he's the son of Mother's friend. Is Alannah seeing him?"

Trenton ran a hand down his face. "No. I think she realized he wasn't right for her, but the flirting was a little ridiculous in my opinion."

Cyrus folded his hands on the desk. "So this Connor person, you think he's the same?"

"I don't know. She won't let me meet him. I can't evaluate him if I don't meet him, but at least with a background check I can find out for sure if there's anything wrong with him."

Cyrus assessed him in an oddly close way. "Why won't she let you meet him?"

"She said I scare men away," Trenton mumbled. He rubbed the back of his neck again. He needed a massage. Lately he carried a lot of tension in the neck and shoulders.

"I see." Loaded words for sure.

Trenton, who'd been staring out the expansive windows, swung his gaze to his brother. "What do you see?" Cyrus was very perceptive, and his ability to analyze served him well as head of the family business. Trenton's stomach knotted in apprehension of his brother's next words.

"Let me ask you this—why are you so worked up about the men she's seeing and the way she's dressing?"

"I'm always concerned about the men in her life. You know that."

"I do, but maybe this new man is her type."

"I'll be the judge of that," Trenton bit out.

Cyrus chuckled knowingly and leaned back in his chair. A spark entered his eyes, as if he'd learned something new. "You can't tell her what to do or who to see."

"Like hell I can't."

"You realize you're abnormally upset and protective over her."

"There's nothing abnormal about it," Trenton said. "She's protective of me, too. We're best friends and she's like a sister to me."

"I've never seen you act this way over Ivy."

"Ivy's older and was married once before. It's different with her. Lana's more like a little sister."

"You're not acting like a big brother, Trent. You're acting very possessive. She's not yours."

"She *is*—" He stopped. The unfinished sentence hung in the air.

Cyrus just looked at him, waiting.

Trenton dialed back his tone. "Are you going to help me or not?"

Cyrus pursed his lips thoughtfully. "Be careful, Trent. Think about what you're doing and where you're going with your relationship with Lana."

He'd thought about it. He knew exactly what he was doing. "I'm looking out for a friend. Nothing more."

"That's not what I'm talking about," Cyrus said. He rested his forearms on the desk, locking his steady gaze with Trenton's. The penetrating look made Trenton uneasy, but he held it. "Once you cross that line, you can't go back. Lana's not the kind of woman to cross that line with and expect you can just go back to being friends. Do not have sex with her unless you're ready for a commitment."

"Who said anything about having sex?"

Cyrus didn't react. "She's not like these other women who hang on your every word, and even after you stop seeing them don't mind if you call for a hookup every now and again. All your little friends-with-benefits associations don't apply. She's different. You of all people should know that and respect it." The oppressive gravity of Cyrus's lecture hung in the air.

In the past few weeks Trenton had already acknowledged that at least part of the high-level emotions he felt toward Alannah was not solely based on platonic feelings. There was more, much more that he chose not to acknowledge. The rage he'd felt when he saw the software developer touch her bare skin had been the most recent way the point had been hammered home. Something was happening to him—to them both, and by extension, their relationship.

He held his brother's gaze and spoke with the same gravity. "I know she's different, Cyrus. Believe me, I know."

Chapter Twelve

Alannah climbed the stairs with Angel in one hand, cradled against her body, and the phone pressed to her ear.

"What's up?" Terri's bubbly voice bounced through the line.

"I need to talk," Alannah said. She placed the dog on the doggie pillow in the corner and sat at the foot of the bed.

She recounted the conversation she'd had with Trenton yesterday. Terri listened attentively without interrupting, only interjecting noncommittal sounds every now and again. When Alannah finished, she asked Terri what she thought.

"About what?"

"About what I told you. Were you listening?"

"Of course I was listening, but Alannah, what are you supposed to do? Your life does not revolve around Trenton Johnson."

"Maybe I should have called him back on Friday night. You don't think I was too mean, do you?"

"You were on a *date*." Terri sighed. "Look, I've told you before that I think you and Trenton have some kind of weird codependency thing going on."

"Is that a yes or no?"

"That's a no, honey." Her voice gentled. "You shouldn't feel guilty about spending time with another man, and he does not have to screen your boyfriends."

"I know." Alannah plucked at the sheet. "It's just that he comes across as this confident, outgoing guy, but he's really sensitive."

"I'm sure he'd love to hear that," Terri said dryly.

Alannah smiled. No, he wouldn't. "He's always been there for me. I don't want to hurt him or make him feel as if he's not important to me anymore."

"Just because he beat up some boys on the playground for you over twenty years ago doesn't mean you owe him for the rest of your life."

"That's not exactly what happened."

"So my details about the story are a little off." Terri let out an exasperated sigh. "Tell you what, let him meet Connor. Hey, what do I know? I still think you're doing the right thing, but if you're not comfortable with it, do what you always do and let him sabotage your relationship."

"He doesn't sabotage my relationships," Alannah said, even though she'd practically accused Trenton of the same thing. "Everything he does is out of love, and he's always been there for me."

"And you've always been there for him. It's a two-way street. Am I wrong?"

"No."

"Okay, then. The scales in this relationship are not tipped in his favor, and real friends don't keep track anyway." The doorbell in Terri's apartment rang and she started moving around. "I've gotta run, sweetie. I have a date, but I can stay on the phone a little longer if you want."

She wasn't surprised Terri had a date in the middle of the week. They both lived such different lives. "No, take care of your company."

"You're not doing anything wrong," Terri said firmly. "Do not feel guilty."

"Go get your date."

"Girl, he'll wait. I'm worried about you. Are you sure you're okay?" The doorbell rang again.

"Yes. Have fun. But Terri?"

"Yes?"

"Do you mind coming with me to The Underground? Trenton's performing this weekend, and it'll be my first time going there…you know, all dolled up. I'm a little nervous." Alannah let out a shaky, embarrassed laugh.

"Honey, of course I don't mind. Besides, I'm dying to see Trenton perform, and it sounds like a cool place to hang out."

"It is. You'll like it."

"We'll touch base later this week so I'll know what time to meet you there, okay? Smooches!"

Alannah hung up and then dragged herself from the bed and undressed. She pulled a pair of Trenton's boxers from the dresser and then paused. She stared at them—black, with vertical red stripes.

Her heart constricted. What was she doing? Wearing his clothes would not help her get over him.

She shoved the underwear back into the bottom of the drawer and removed a white chemise, something new and sexy she'd purchased but hadn't worn yet. She put that on instead.

"Good night, Angel," she whispered. The dog's head popped up and then settled down onto her paws again.

Alannah slipped under the covers and pulled the comforter up to her chin. Not surprisingly, she didn't fall asleep. She had Trenton on the brain.

She loved him so much, too much, and wished she had the courage to cut him off, but slicing off a foot would be easier and less painful.

Rolling onto her side, she closed her eyes.

Her love for him had probably started the first day they'd met, although she'd only been eight years old, and the circumstances hadn't been ideal…

****

Traipsing across the grass, Alannah enviously watched the other children running, sliding, and swinging. She hated recess because she didn't have any friends at this new private school. But at least she had her books. The three in her arms had been checked out from the school library this morning. She'd always loved to read, but it had become even more important and allowed her to escape from this new life her parents had forced her into. Each day at the new school proved hard and hadn't gotten any easier. She didn't belong, and the other kids never let her forget.

Before she could get to the benches on the other side of the yard, three boys approached.

"What you got there, four eyes?"

"More books?"

She stared straight ahead, her steps less exuberant, less confident. She didn't bother anyone and couldn't understand why they constantly picked on her.

Clutching the books to her chest, she recalled the words her parents had told her to repeat. *Sticks and stones may break my bones but words will never hurt me.*

Two of the boys planted themselves in front of her, arms folded, and blocked her progress. Alannah skidded to a halt. Eyes on the ground, she turned slowly back toward the building. She'd read inside today.

The biggest boy, the main bully, knocked the books from her arms. "You don't belong here."

Her belly quivered with fear. He'd never done that before.

His actions emboldened the other two to circle.

"Why are you here, four eyes? You're poor."

"Are you on *welfare*?" one taunted.

"Did you see the car her father drives?" The main bully laughed loud and mean. "It's a *Toyota*. And it's old."

The other two joined in the laughter, and Alannah's cheeks burned red.

She didn't understand much, but her parents had explained that because of her good grades and the test she'd taken, the school had given her a full tuition scholarship. "Otherwise, we couldn't have afforded to send you to such a prestigious school," her mother had said, her voice filled with pride. So the kids were right—she didn't belong there.

"Cat got your tongue, freckle face?" one of the boys asked.

Alannah kept her eyes on the books strewn open on the grass. The colorful images of a rainbow and ponies stared up at the blue sky from one of them. The other two had fallen open and specks of dirt marred the words on the stark white pages.

She didn't know what to do. Should she stay quiet? Should she speak? There were three of them and only one of her.

Someone shoved her from behind, and the blow knocked her to her hands and knees and ripped off her glasses. Other kids approached, boys and girls. They giggled and pointed at her.

"What's she doing down there?"

More giggles.

This incident was the last straw in a string of incidents that finally broke her young spirit. Head hanging low, Alannah felt her face get mottled and redden. Tears filled her eyes.

"Aw, look at her, she's gonna cry."

Even more laughter.

"Leave her alone!" A loud voice broke through the jeers and laughter with authority.

An immediate hush fell over the small group of tormenters, and Alannah looked up to see her savior, just a kid himself. His green eyes were so vivid, she could see them clearly even through the curtain of tears. The kids all stared at him in shock, eyes wide and mouths hanging open.

"He's talking," a girl whispered. What a weird thing to say. Why wouldn't he be talking?

Her hero stomped toward the leader of the bullies and shoved him hard. The boy stumbled back into his friends.

"What are you looking at? Get out of here! If you ever pick on a girl again, I'll kick your ass."

The children gasped, and the bullies scattered, one of them calling out for a teacher. "Miss Brown! Miss Brown! Trenton Johnson said a bad word."

A hand came down into Alannah's line of vision. Gratefully, she took it and was pulled to her feet.

The boy handed her the glasses, and she brushed dirt off the lenses. Luckily they weren't scratched, so she slipped them on.

"Are you okay?" the boy asked. He was really cute, but his hair was long, with thick, loose curls that attacked his ears and neck, as if his parents hadn't taken him for a haircut in at least a year.

Alannah nodded. "Yes, I'm okay," she answered in a quivering voice, still a bit shaken and unsure of what exactly had happened or what to do next. It still amazed her that someone had come to her defense.

"You need to go to the nurse." He eyed her skinned knee.

She hadn't even realized she'd been hurt, but the sight of the bruising and blood sent a signal of stinging pain to her brain. She winced.

"I'm Trenton, but you can call me Trent."

"I'm Alannah," she said softly.

A few of the kids still hovered nearby, staring, but he didn't seem to notice. Since he ignored them, so did she.

"Come on," he said. "And don't worry, I won't let anybody mess with you again."

Holding her books in one arm, he took her hand in his. Then he led the way across the playground, and she followed.

****

Alannah sighed into the quiet darkness of her room. Since then, she and Trenton had been almost inseparable. Mr. and Mrs. Johnson, thrilled she had accomplished what the best therapists hadn't been able to—get Trenton to talk again—invited her family to parties and on vacations to exotic locations. By the time she finished middle school, her parents allowed her to go without them on trips overseas with the Johnsons, and she more or less became a part of their mega-wealthy family.

But when puberty hit, Alannah couldn't help but notice more and more of Trenton's physical attributes. His muscular build. The cute way he smiled, with his mouth tilted up to the right. Even at that young age, she recognized that the queasiness in her belly whenever he came around had nothing to do with friendship. She'd fallen in love with her best friend.

By college, the occasional erotic dream about him had her waking up in a tangle of sheets with the area between her legs moist and throbbing. Alarmed though she'd been by the wetness in her panties, she'd fingered herself to thoughts of him more times than she could count, imagining that he watched her with the same lustful eyes the way he did other girls.

She came to love him so much that being with him made her hurt, but being without him was so much worse. So she put up with the queasiness in her belly and the ache in chest, since they were the lesser of two evils.

Because…she simply couldn't fathom life without Trenton.

Chapter Thirteen

"Terri's going to meet us at The Underground," Alannah said from the bathroom where she was getting dressed.

Trenton halted his prowl across the floor of her bedroom. "She's a bad influence." He had no doubt Terri was the driving force behind much of Alannah's changes and desire to *stand out.*

"You sound like somebody's grandfather," Alannah called. "She's not a bad influence. She's my friend, and I have a mind of my own, thank you very much."

He stuffed his hands into the pockets of his khakis. "If you say so."

"While you're on stage she'll keep me company at the table."

Trenton checked the time. "Are you almost ready?"

"You're really in a mood tonight."

The cause of his bad mood was the sizable slab of dread in his stomach as he anticipated what Alannah would wear. The longer she stayed in the bathroom, the more apprehensive he became.

Finally, she came out, hand at the back holding the edges of the sleeveless thing—he really couldn't even call it a dress—together. The plunging neckline showed hints of her small, plump breasts, and the hem hugged her thighs several inches above the knees.

And it was red. Red for fire. Red for sexy. Red for sultry.

Alannah strutted over in a pair of heels that made her hips roll when she walked, and she turned around just in front of him. "Would you zip me up?"

His gaze dropped and he noticed how the stretchy fabric accentuated her behind. Because of the plunging neckline, she didn't have on a bra, and he wondered if she even wore panties. He couldn't see any below the zipper line.

He gulped and shifted from one foot to the other as heat filled his groin. "When did you get this?"

"I saw it in a magazine and ordered it online. I can't believe how well it fits."

Trenton swiped at the beads of sweat that popped out on his forehead. His funny, mousy friend had turned into a brazen, shapely sexpot who had his imagination going wild with all the things he could do to her.

With trembling fingers, he silently closed the dress and covered the creamy skin of her back.

"What do you think?" She turned in a circle. "If you were a guy—"

"Would you stop with the 'if I was a guy' crap?" Trenton snapped in a flash of anger.

"I'm kidding. Sheesh." She frowned. "Seriously, though, would you notice me if you didn't know me?" She placed both hands on her hips.

He liked her much better in glasses and the shapeless grays and beiges she used to wear. Ivy had been right. The beauty of her eyes was more visible now, but so was every bend and arc of her body for other men to notice. And they'd notice. Especially in a place like where they were headed.

"Your dress is ridiculously short and tight. *Everybody* at The Underground is going to notice you."

"Thank you." She smiled happily and ran her fingers through the heavy, silky sheath of hair around her face.

"It wasn't a compliment." Trenton scowled.

"I know, but I choose to take it as one. Let's go, Mr. Grumpy. I hope you get into a better mood or you're going to spoil my night."

She hooked an arm around his and they exited the room together. Her cheery mood only made him surlier, and on the way out the front door he recognized why.

She was glowing, and downright *excited* to show her ass tonight.

****

When they arrived at The Underground, Trenton took Alannah's hand. She held on tight, standing right behind him and watching the back of his head as he signaled to the guy at the door. He looked great in a plaid shirt with a solid vest and khakis. In the Range Rover, he'd donned an English riding cap and completed the ensemble. No red-blooded heterosexual woman would be able to resist him tonight.

As soon as the doorman saw Trenton, he waved them forward and they were immediately admitted entrance, past the customers waiting outside.

The dark club was already jumping and filled with people who'd arrived for hip-hop night, which tended to draw an especially large crowd. For diehard rap fans, this was the only place to be in Seattle tonight.

Trenton's mood noticeably improved upon entrance. His head bounced to the warmup act, a group singing a cover of a popular R&B hit, and his tense shoulders visibly relaxed. He walked through like a movie star, shaking hands and letting people touch him. This was his world.

The venue was designed to look like a basement, with exposed brick walls and pipes running along the ceilings. The two bars on either side were packed with customers placing orders or idling over drinks.

Trenton led her through the crowd, which was not an easy feat. He constantly stopped to give dap to male acquaintances and hug women dressed in skimpy attire that made Alannah's outfit look like an ensemble fit for the North Pole.

As they moved through the club, Alannah imagined a situation where Trenton held her hand because he wanted the men and women there to know they belonged to each other. Involuntarily, her hand tightened on his and he paused to look back at her, eyebrows raised in question.

"Nothing," she said, smiling reassuringly.

He started forward again. Carving a path through the throng of bodies, they arrived at his usual table, which afforded a good view of the stage, and sat in two of the four seats.

They ordered drinks while they waited for Terri, and of course women came over to speak to Trenton, like always, as if Alannah wasn't even sitting there. To his credit, he made sure the women acknowledged her, but otherwise, she was as invisible as a speck of lint on white sheets. They were always polite, but their tight-lipped smiles made it obvious they'd prefer if she left.

"Where's your girl?" Trenton asked when they were finally alone. He sipped from a bottle of Full Moon beer, the only beer served in the venue. She'd have one alcoholic beverage, maybe two, because she couldn't hold her liquor. A shortcoming he loved to tease her about. "I don't want to leave you until she gets here."

"Don't know." Alannah took a peek at her phone but didn't see any missed calls from Terri. "She should have been here by now. I hope she's okay." This was late, even for Terri.

A few minutes later she spotted her friend at the far end, having just walked in the door. She saw Alannah and hurried toward them in a pair of skintight jeans and an equally tight halter top. She'd removed the braids and now wore her hair in a layered blond bob. Just about every man she passed on the way to the table ogled her as she walked by. A couple even grabbed her hand and whispered in her ear, but she didn't detour from her destination.

When Terri arrived at the table, Alannah stood and gave her a tight squeeze, relieved. "I thought you weren't coming."

"Would you believe I got a flat tire?" Terri's red lips flattened in annoyance. "Luckily I know how to change one, but it messed up my brand new manicure." She pouted and examined her chipped nails.

"Hey, Terri." Trenton came around the table to give her a hug, too.

At one time Alannah had worried that Trenton had been attracted to her friend. But either he wasn't attracted to her or he hid it extremely well, because he treated her exactly the way he treated Alannah—like a platonic friend. For that she was grateful. It would have been devastating if her two friends had hooked up.

"Hi, Trent. Can't wait to see your performance tonight."

"Thanks. You're in for a treat." It wasn't vanity. He really was good. "I'll leave you ladies alone. See you later." He strolled off toward one of the bars.

Alannah sat down and Terri took the seat beside her. Leaning in, her friend asked, "Is he still acting like a jerk?"

"He's calmed down, thank goodness. Although he had a couple of moments earlier tonight."

"Well, you look fabulous." Terri's gaze flicked over Alannah. "That dress is like…pow!"

Alannah smiled. She pulled on the hem, a little self-conscious. "You really think so?"

"Honey, you're going to have to beat them off with a stick tonight."

Alannah preened under the encouraging words, particularly since Trenton hadn't offered a word of praise about her appearance.

"So," Terri said, taking a deep breath and looking around. "Who do I have to blow to get a drink around here?"

Alannah laughed. Her friend's irreverent sense of humor and I-don't-care attitude were refreshing. "I don't think that will be necessary." She waved over the waitress.

The club continued to fill up, and before long, the waitress came back and mentioned a light-skinned man at the bar wanted to buy Terri a drink.

Terri followed the line of the server's pointing finger. "Cu-ute. And he's tall. I like my men tall." She arched a brow at Alannah. "He's got a friend."

Alannah noticed the friend, too, but he was preoccupied with the performance on the stage, while Terri's potential stared right at them.

Terri sent a finger wave over to the guy and leaned toward the waitress. "Tell him I would love a drink, but he'll have to get one for my friend, too."

Alannah's eyes widened. "No, don't do that."

Terri waved her off and placed an order.

"And you?" the waitress asked Alannah.

"Nothing for me, thanks."

"Get her a strawberry daiquiri."

"Terri."

"Thank you." Terri waved away the waitress and leaned toward Alannah. "Stop worrying. It's no big deal."

"He offered *you* a drink, not me."

"Same difference. You're sitting with me, so you reap the benefits."

Although Alannah appreciated the move, she cringed inwardly at having to coerce someone into buying her a drink.

The night couldn't possibly get any worse.

CHAPTER FOURTEEN

Trenton leaned back against the bar, beer bottle in hand. His Kappa Alpha Sigma brother and owner of The Underground, Devin, stood beside him. When Devin had explained the concept of the club, Trenton had fronted a huge chunk of the money needed to open the place, all of which had already been repaid with interest.

On stage, the lead singer of a four-member band sang "Don't Leave Me" by Backstreet, which had been preceded by "On Bended Knee" by Boyz II Men.

Devin stroked his goatee. "Begging asses. No woman will ever have my nose that wide open to have me begging like that."

"I hear you." Trenton took a swig of beer. "Keith Sweat was the worst, wasn't he?"

"He was bad, but the whole idea of begging a woman started with The Temptations—talking about ain't too proud to beg." Devin shook his head in disgust. "Ain't a woman alive could make me beg, that's for sure."

He raised his bottle and Trenton touched his against it.

"Amen."

They stood in silence, listening to the musicians on stage. As the emcee asked the audience to give a round of applause to the departing act, three of Trenton's Kappa Alpha brothers walked up with another man he didn't recognize.

He and his fraternity brothers greeted each other with the customary handshake. Then Julian, dark-skinned and with a low-cut fade, placed a hand on the fourth person with them, a stocky, brown-skinned guy with a circle beard. "This is a buddy of mine, Steve. He's visiting from Las Vegas."

"Welcome," Trenton said. He and Devin introduced themselves. "I was in Vegas not too long ago."

"I know," Steve said. A one-sided grin transformed his face into a knowing smirk. "Heard all about it. The honey you were with was real nice-looking, man. Real nice."

Trenton chuckled. Not one to kiss and tell, he kept his response brief. "She's a lot of fun." Beth had very much appreciated the trip and shown him multiple times over the weekend exactly how much.

Steve used his chin to point across the club. "The one in the red mini—that you, too, bruh?"

Trenton's eyes went in the direction he'd indicated, straight to the table where Alannah and Terri sat huddled together in conversation. His relaxed pose tightened a smidgen, and after a slight hesitation, he answered. "Yeah, that's me."

Steve bit his lip. "Damn."

Bristling and shoulders tight, Trenton paid closer attention to this newcomer.

Devin patted Steve on the back and laughed out loud. "Trenton gets all the fine honeys. That's why his line name is Loverman." He and a couple of the other guys broke into a few bars of Shabba Ranks' "Mr. Loverman."

Trenton relaxed and laughed at the friendly ribbing. "It's not my fault I have better lines than you suckers."

A chorus of oohs and ahs filled the small group.

"You're a lucky man," Steve continued, keeping his eyes on the women. "The one you took to Vegas was fine, but this girl…she's got that sweet look about her. Must be one of them nice girls, a lady in the street but a freak in the sheets." He laughed knowingly.

Trenton frowned. Was this guy for real? "Why you still looking at her?"

Steve turned to him and raised his eyebrows. "What, a brother can't look?"

"Come on, Steve," Julian said.

An unnatural silence fell over the group. The chatter and sounds of the thumping music receded as Trenton gave the newcomer his undivided attention.

"You believe this fool?" he asked no one in particular. He deposited the beer on the bar behind him with a thunk and stood up straight, almost a full head above Steve. His muscles quivered with tension. "Nah, a brother can't look. I told you that's me right there, and you looking at her like you want to fuck her or something. That's disrespectful."

"I wasn't trying to be disrespectful, man." Steve laughed uneasily, his eyes traveling through the group of friends. He sought backup, but none of them gave the encouragement he wanted, so he found it in himself. "You should be proud you have a woman who catches the eye of other men."

"You need to keep your motherfucking eyes to yourself."

"Are you serious, man?" Steve laughed, this time with more bravado. Again he searched the group for backing, but their grave expressions offered none. "It's not like I approached her. She sitting way over there—"

"Get him the fuck out of here." Trenton's fingers folded into a fist, and he dismissed the conversation by turning his back on Steve instead of punching the idiot in the face.

Two of his frat brothers immediately stepped on either side of Steve. Each grabbed an arm and started escorting him out.

As they hauled him away, Trenton heard him holler, "This is some bullshit!"

"Fuck him," Devin muttered, resting an elbow on the bar. "You all right?"

Trenton flexed his fingers. Only the thought of bad publicity and a potential lawsuit held him in check. "I'm fine." He reclaimed his beer and let his eyes veer to where Alannah and Terri sat, heads still close together and whispering.

"I didn't know he was such an asshole." Julian grimaced.

"Everybody knows Alannah is off limits, and I told him. Don't know why he asked you that question in the first place."

Trenton slanted a look at his frat brother. "So he just wanted to start something?"

"Pretty much."

"No damn respect."

"I hear you."

****

Everyone liked hip-hop night, but they *loved* when Trenton took the stage. On the nights he performed, The Underground skirted the boundaries of the fire code. Watching the billionaire musician from one of America's most prestigious families get up on stage with his keyboardist and drummer was a must-see.

When it was almost time for Trenton to perform, Alannah watched Devin step up to the mic. "I know why you're here, but I'm not sure you're ready for him."

The audience went crazy, screaming and yelling.

Devin laughed, clearly enjoying the energy in the room. "You sure? You sure you're ready for this?"

"We're ready!"

"Bring him out!"

"All right then," Devin said. "Give it up for my boy, my frat, Mr. Loverman himself, Trenton Johnson!"

The audience went wild. Wide-eyed, Terri turned to Alannah, surprised at the crowd's reaction.

"Watch this," Alannah mouthed.

The lights in the venue went down and a hushed silence fell over the crowd. Very low, the first track came on, supported by the soft beat of the bass drum and the keyboardist's fingers trailing across the keys. As the sounds of the music grew louder, a spotlight appeared, positioned on Trenton's bare, tatted back. The screaming started up again and reached an eardrum-busting level.

Alannah clapped her hands and moved to the beat with the rest of the audience. As they danced, the music became even louder. Beneath his cap, which he'd throw into the audience at the end of the performance, Trenton's head bounced in time to the melody.

All of a sudden, the hip-hop track exploded, and he swung around with a violin positioned on his collarbone, and dragged the bow across the strings. The crowd yelled as a unique rendition of Fat Joe's "Lean Back" played out before them, and as he smoothly transitioned to "LoveHate Thing" by Wale, Trenton became lost in the music.

He danced, taking full advantage of the stage, lean hips swaying and muscles flexing as he moved. He winked at women in the audience or dropped to one knee and strummed out the notes like the lead guitarist in a rock band. Concentrating on the chords of each song, his fingers slid along the neck of the violin and produced a full range of vibrato movements.

Alannah could easily have been one of the women screaming and yelling, because her mouth went dry as she watched Trenton command the stage. Shirtless, ripped abs on display and hard biceps flexing, he played the tunes with jab-like strokes. Hypnotized by the sounds of the stringed instrument and his swaying hips, Alannah trailed a finger down the side of her damp neck.

The drag and wail of the violin, the beat of the drum, and the notes of the keyboard invited people to dance. They danced around tables. They danced standing along the walls.

Then Trenton stopped, dead silence. His signature move. Bouncing, he counted, and the crowd chanted with him, "One, two, one, two, three, four…"

He dived back in, dropped to his knees in a back bend and slowly rose while the bow moved in a furious back-and-forth motion, signaling the finale of the song. Alannah and Terri jumped to their feet with the other audience members, clapping and whooping at the top of their lungs.

"Wow," Terri mouthed, wide-eyed.

Once the raucous cheering ended, the stage lights dimmed and focused on Trenton. He ended the set the way he always did, with a slowed-down rendition of Will Smith's song to his oldest son, "Just the Two of Us."

No matter how many times Alannah saw him perform the melody, she had the same reaction as if it was the first time. Tears moistened her eyes, because she knew, better than anyone else there, the full story of Trenton's past, why this song was so important to him, and why he'd learned to play the violin.

Playing made him feel closer to his father, a classically trained violinist who had taken leave from the Johnson family business to pursue his passion for music. He'd toured with a pit orchestra and carried musical theatre to audiences all over the world.

Alannah knew the pain Trenton carried behind the smile, understood the markings on his skin were more than art, and his body more than a canvas. The images of a snake, of flames, Philadelphia landmarks, musical notes, and every single illustration etched into his flesh did double duty. They hid the pain of a seven-year-old boy and gave him something to talk about, instead of the scars that marred his flesh.

She could almost believe Trenton channeled his father's spirit while on stage. He didn't perform because of ego or because he needed the adoration of the crowded club. He performed to pay homage to his hero. He performed because he loved music, and because playing the violin made him feel close to his father, taken from him suddenly, violently, and much too soon.

CHAPTER FIFTEEN

This might officially be the worst night of her life.

When the man who had bought a drink for Terri had come over, Alannah had taken that opportunity to thank him, but he'd been so preoccupied with Terri he barely acknowledged her. The two exchanged numbers, and that was the first of what turned out to be a pattern the entire night.

Men either bought Terri a drink or came by and whispered in her friend's ear. Alannah declined any other drinks after the first Terri procured for her, and lingered over her daiquiri while her friend took advantage of her popularity to try other options and sample appetizers on the menu.

In truth, her friend was a sight to behold, her ability to flirt an art form. Beside her, Alannah felt like the ugly duckling. Every now and again a man who approached Terri smiled politely at Alannah and then looked away. It was the oddest thing. As if they were afraid to pay her too much attention. As if they wanted to make it abundantly clear they were interested in Terri, not her. Obviously, she was out of her depth. As the night wore on, the inattention crushed her spirits.

"You okay?" Terri asked. She placed a hand on Alannah's bare shoulder.

"I'm fine. Gonna run to the little girls' room." She managed a weak smile and left the table.

Inside the bathroom, she waited her turn, so close to tears she had to gnaw on her upper lip to keep it from trembling. When an empty stall became available, she closed herself inside and stood there, fighting the urge to cry. But a sob broke free and she covered her mouth, shoving back the disheartening feelings.

What an idiot she was. At least before she could blame her lack of prospects on the fact that she used to dress in loose-fitting clothes that hid her figure so well even she couldn't find it. Growing up in a strict household had made her very self-conscious about her body and how she portrayed herself to the male gender.

Modesty, Lana. A young lady should be modest at all times.

Her mother had beaten those words into her head for many years. Into the head of her sisters, too. Nonetheless, her middle sister became pregnant in high school. Even though she lost the baby, the situation at home worsened for Alannah, the youngest. She should have started dating at sixteen, but because of the pregnancy, her parents decided that she had to finish school first.

The new mantra became, *Education first, boys last.* As if she hadn't been pulling straight A's all along.

Alannah looked down at her outfit. The red dress should have been a statement. Hard to believe not one single man in the place found her attractive enough to approach.

She'd even worn heels! She'd practiced in them to make sure she didn't look like a fool tonight, but she looked like a fool anyway. Because no one wanted her.

A lone tear attached to her lash and hung on. She brushed it away, hoping she hadn't ruined her makeup, which, on top of the horrible night, would simply be too much.

Taking a deep breath, Alannah readied to face the rest of the night. She wanted to leave now but couldn't pull Trenton away from all the women falling all over themselves to get to him. She knew all about their aggressive acts because he'd shared them with her before. Women passed him their numbers, and the more assertive ones handed over their panties.

Alannah unlatched the door and went to the mirrored wall. She waited a few minutes until a spot cleared and then went through the motions of washing her hands. In reality, she used the opportunity to examine her reflection. Overall, she looked okay.

Her hair had flattened a bit, but still hung in silky and straight lines around her face. Light makeup added color to her cheeks and she'd accentuated her eyes with liner, mascara, and an eyelash curler. Thankfully, none of the red-toned lipstick had made it onto her teeth, and she'd been careful to sip from a straw the entire night to minimize the loss of color to her lips.

Maybe it was the dress. She examined the outfit with a critical eye. Although it hugged her body, she didn't have a large chest. If she'd stuffed her bra, maybe?

She shook her head. Silly thought. No point in padding her bra, because that would be false advertising. She simply had to accept that there was something about her that didn't attract the men here tonight. The Underground wasn't her element.

Alannah dried her hands on a paper towel and eased past the women crowded around the mirror. She exited the bathroom, still deflated, when a man standing against the wall touched her arm as she passed.

A smooth-as-silk voice arrested her steps. "Why the long face?" Brilliant teeth practically glowed against skin the color of onyx. He had a diamond in each ear and was fine as all get out, with the build of a running back and a tight black shirt to show off his muscles.

"I have a long face?" Alannah pushed away the nervous flutter in her stomach. For the first time tonight someone was paying her attention, and it felt really, really good.

"You sure do. Let me see that smile. I know it's in there somewhere."

Alannah laughed, blushing.

"There it is. Gorgeous."

Another man next to him tapped his shoulder and whispered in his ear. Gradually, the ebony god's expression changed.

"Sorry for bothering you." He smiled again, that polite smile she'd received all evening, and the two men walked away.

Stunned, Alannah didn't move at first. She touched her hair and surreptitiously breathed into her palm. Men had seldom noticed the old Alannah, but now, even when they did, they behaved as if there was something wrong with her.

What the hell was going on?

She walked back to the table where Terri sat entertaining two of her minions. Both men stood when Alannah arrived, and with a few words of goodbye, they left her and Terri alone again.

Her friend danced in the seat, wiggling her body in a snakelike manner to the current performer's thumping beat and rap lyrics.

Alannah leaned toward her friend and softly asked, "Do I look okay?"

Terri looked at her, but continued to dance. "Of course. I would've told you if you didn't. Why?"

With anyone else, Alannah might have been too embarrassed to admit this, but she had to say it. "No one will talk to me."

Terri stopped her gyrations and frowned. "You mean men?"

Alannah swallowed, face coloring. "Yes." She told Terri about the incident outside the bathroom.

"Pfft. His friend must have reminded him he had a wife and kids at home. You probably dodged a bullet."

That didn't explain the lack of attention during the entire night.

"I guess." Tears crept to the corners of her eyes again, but Alannah blinked them away. "I just thought…I dunno." She stared at her watered-down drink.

Terri squeezed her wrist. "It's not you, okay? Really. Sometimes it's like that. Some nights you can't get a number. Other times men hound you, no matter what you look like. I can't tell you how many times I've been in a store with a baseball cap, sweats, and tennis shoes on, and men approach me. It's a crapshoot. You're having a slow night, that's all."

"Do you have slow nights?" She already knew Terri didn't, and when her friend bit her top lip and didn't respond, it confirmed that Terri had only made those comments to be nice.

Jealousy stung Alannah's belly, followed quickly by the heat of shame that she was even jealous of her friend.

Alannah signaled for the waitress.

The young woman hustled over. "Another daiquiri?"

Alannah gave her a strong and friendly smile, despite her crushed spirits. "No. This time I'll take a rum and Coke, please."

Terri watched her sideways but didn't comment.

Alannah wouldn't listen anyway. She didn't care anymore. The night officially sucked, and she wanted to feel better.

CHAPTER SIXTEEN

"I'm fine, I'm fine." Eyes half closed and speech slurred, Alannah waved Trenton away with an overly dramatic gesture and then slumped across the table.

Mouth tight, he stared at her. She looked about to slide out of the chair onto the floor.

Fuming, he scanned the club for her so-called friend, Terri, and caught her eye when she looked up from chatting up some guy against the wall behind the tables.

She excused herself and came over.

"She's drunk," he said, barely containing his anger.

"I'm not thrunk," Alannah slurred.

Trenton glared at Terri. "Some friend you are. How many drinks did she have?"

"I don't know. Is she going to be all right?" Terri tilted her head to get a good look at Alannah.

"I'll make sure that she is," he said. "Because that's what friends do." He looped an arm around Alannah's narrow waist and helped her to her feet. She leaned heavily against him.

"I'm sorry," Terri said, concern etched in her features.

"I'm taking her out of here." Trenton tossed another disgusted look at Terri, who bit her bottom lip in distress. He then tightened the supporting arm around Alannah's waist and halfway carried her through the crowded club.

In the parking lot, he struggled to get her into the car, but managed to set her in the seat and secure the seatbelt across her lap. The drive to her apartment was made in silence because she dozed off and on the entire way. Once there, he parked in the driveway and unlocked the door before walking back to his vehicle.

He lifted her out of the Range Rover, and her head flopped backward. Trenton clenched his jaw and hoisted her higher in his arms. When he kicked the front door shut behind him, Angel poked her head out of the cage and growled low in her throat.

"I'm *helping* her," he hissed, annoyed he even cared what that damn dog thought.

Angel only growled louder. Trenton walked on by, the trek up the stairs not an easy one under Alannah's dead weight. Inside her bedroom, he dropped her in an inelegant pile on the bed in the dark room.

"Where am I?" she muttered, rolling onto her stomach, butt in the air.

"Home," Trenton bit out. "I'll be right back. Stay right there."

"I'm not going anywhere," she mumbled into the mattress.

Trenton went downstairs to the kitchen and endured more threatening sounds from Angel. He poured a glass of water and rushed back up the stairs and into the bathroom.

"What are you doing?" Alannah called from the bedroom.

"Getting you some aspirin. Don't move."

He scanned the medicine cabinet and found an almost empty bottle of aspirin. He checked the expiration date first and then emptied a couple of the tablets into his palm.

Back in the bedroom, he flipped on the lamp beside the bed and assessed the scene before him. Alannah had dozed off again in the same position he'd left her in—face down and the red mini hiked up high enough for him to see the bottom curve of her bare ass.

An ass made for spanking.

His penis jumped and he swallowed hard. Flushing guiltily, he removed her shoes and she stirred awake.

Trenton lowered onto the bed beside her. "Here, take these. They'll help so you don't feel too crappy in the morning."

She wrinkled her nose, moaned, and turned away. "What is it?"

"Aspirin. Take them." She'd never been drunk before. At the most, tipsy. She had no idea the hangover she'd experience in the morning thanks to her binge at the club. "Drink all the water, too."

He force-fed her the aspirin and the entire glass of water. She coughed a little and he cradled her in the curve of his arm. A thin stream of water trickled from the corner of her mouth onto her dress, but he made sure she drank every bit from the glass.

"Okay?" Trenton said when she'd finished. He set the glass on the table beside the bed.

"Mhmm."

Then Alannah did something he could never have anticipated. She wrapped her arms around his neck and pulled him down on top of her. Before he could even compute that they were strewn across the mattress, she turned her face into his neck and inhaled. "You always smell so good."

The sensation of her soft lips made his blood pressure spike, and he held his breath and closed his eyes as he fought within himself. She didn't make the struggle any easier when she licked his neck, a long, slow movement from his shoulder all the way up to right below his ear—the moist sensation making his heart beat double time. "Taste good, too."

His stomach and fingers squeezed into a mass of tight knots. "Lana…"

"Guess what color my panties are," she whispered hotly in his ear.

His thigh muscles constricted so tight blood surely ceased to flow below his knees. "I'm not going to guess—"

"Red, to match my dress."

Shit.

"It's actually a thong, with cute little bows on each hip. Wanna see?"

Yes.

"Lana, sweetheart, you're drunk," Trenton said, voice taut and strained. Could she hear how hard this was for him? He attempted to extricate himself from her clinging arms, but she tightened her hold.

"Love you so much," she whispered, pressing soft lips to his cheek.

His abs clenched so tight that long seconds passed before he breathed oxygen again. It wasn't the first time she'd ever told him she loved him. They'd said those words to each other plenty of times over the years, because they did love each other. But having her say those words, kiss his cheek, and lie strewn across her bed had unexpected consequences in his pants.

"Okay, enough." Steely resolve filled his voice. Trenton pulled her with him when he sat up, but he tore her arms from around his neck. She fell back onto the mattress but bounced right back up and straddled his lap.

She gasped, hazel eyes lighting up mischievously. "Well, well, well, what have we here?" One hand covered his crotch and squeezed. A flash of heat accosted his groin and he instantaneously grew harder and elongated.

Trenton groaned and grabbed her roaming hand. Gritting his teeth, he fought for control. "Behave yourself."

"I want to see it," she pleaded, mouth close to his. "The famous serpent. The *Womb Beater.*"

And he wanted to show it to her.

Years ago, he'd briefly dated a model. After the relationship ended, she told a magazine he was so well endowed that she'd felt as if he'd beaten her womb every time they'd had sex. Shortly thereafter, the nickname Womb Beater emerged in the tabloids and the gossip blogs.

When at first women had chased him because of his wealth and good looks, curiosity was added to the mix. They wanted to know if it was true, and some of his sexual partners had even tried to sneak and take pictures to provide proof of his size.

"You don't want to see it," Trenton said.

"Please," she said petulantly, with a cute little pout. She twisted and wiggled against him in an effort to break free and make another grab for the front of his pants. "I want to see if it's true. I've known you forever and I've never seen it—not even a glimpse."

And then Alannah pressed her mouth to his. Trenton froze, taken completely by surprise, and his heart rate tore into a full sprint.

Her lips were soft and pliable. She moaned, and that sound alone tipped him over the edge and destroyed the last milligram of his restraint. He seized her hips and hauled her tight against his crotch. His hard loins filled with heat and a pulsing, throbbing desire that had him focused only on tasting more and more of her.

Dipping his tongue into the warmth of her mouth, he greedily sampled the unfamiliar flavor of the sweet depths, devouring her lips like a man deprived of the basic sustenance necessary for survival. She opened wider, kissing him back with an equal amount of enthusiasm and relish.

Her fingers raked across his scalp and sent a line of shivers dashing down his spine. Trenton's left hand clamped around her like a vise, crushing her into his hard chest. Slipping his other hand under her dress, he captured the slender piece of fabric that held the thong together. He brushed his thumb across the little bow and gave an experimental tug.

Alannah moaned again and he kissed her harder, curling his fingers around the thin strip of cloth. He wanted to see it. He wanted to drag it down her thighs with his teeth. Raging hunger charged through him, his only thought to tear off the flimsy barrier and assuage the urgent, unstoppable need that had taken him to the brink of insanity over the past six weeks.

The devil on his shoulder urged him to go for it. The angel on the other shoulder warned she wasn't in her right mind.

Alas, common sense prevailed. She was drunk. She didn't know what she was doing.

Trenton severed contact with her mouth and drew in a harsh, painful breath.

"Don't stop," Alannah whimpered.

She leaned in to re-establish the kiss, and he pushed her off his lap. She fell backward onto the bed with her legs wide open, and he pinned her hands above her head, careful not to press his hips against hers, no matter how badly he craved the contact.

"Why'd you stop?" she moaned, making it difficult for him to be a decent human being.

"Listen to me: *you're drunk*. I'm going to leave you alone now, so you can sleep this off."

He jumped up quickly and stumbled backward off the bed so she couldn't grab him again.

"No, wait." Alannah stretched a hand. "Don't go. Don't leave me alone."

She looked so pitiful lying there, hair splayed out on the sheets like a high crown of red flames, her eyes at half-mast in her drunken state.

Breathing was difficult for Trenton, coming in short, arduous spurts. Whether from the physical exertion of fighting her or from fighting his body, he couldn't be sure.

Keeping ironclad control on his voice, Trenton said, "If I stay, you have to behave yourself."

"I will."

"Promise me," he said in a hard tone.

"I promise. I pinky promise." She held up the little finger of her right hand.

Trenton took a few more deep breaths and ran shaky fingers over his head. If she attacked him again, he was getting the hell out of there.

Against his better judgment, he eased onto the bed, keeping an eye on Alannah in case she made any sudden moves.

"Thank you," she murmured. She curled up next to him and placed her head on his chest.

Trenton ran a hand over his face and breathed easier. He fished his public phone out of his pocket and turned it off. That way the girl who'd caught his hat at The Underground, whom he'd planned to see later, wouldn't disturb them if she called to check his whereabouts.

"Trenton?"

He tensed. He thought she'd fallen asleep. "Yeah?"

"Do you think I'm pretty?" Her voice wobbled, the question pitched in hurt. What had prompted her to ask such a thing?

Pretty didn't begin to describe her. Such a paltry word was

insufficient, because he didn't find only her exterior appealing. She was lovely on the inside, too. Alannah was the only woman outside of family who ever gave him any gifts of substance. Other women lamented about what to give a man who had everything and then offered him sex—something he could have anyway, anytime, almost anywhere.

Alannah, on the other hand, put thought into her gifts. Like the engraved handcrafted violin stand she'd had created for his birthday once. "Now you can put your dad's violin on display," she'd said. For years he'd kept his father's instrument protected in its case, but now it held a place of prominence in his music room, where he could see it every time he practiced.

"Of course." He stroked her hair, smoothing the strands with a careful, tender touch. "You're the most beautiful woman I know."

That seemed to satisfy her. She melted against him and flung an arm across his chest, as if to prevent his escape when she fell into deep sleep. Soon her gentle snoring could be heard.

Hopefully he could finally get some sleep, too. Trenton turned off the lamp and relaxed into the pillows, yet he couldn't stop thinking about the fact that he was lying in bed with Alannah. He shouldn't be so aroused, but the more he thought about the current situation, the more his body betrayed him. She fit against him perfectly, her pliable body tucked into his side like a rib. Like she belonged there.

Luckily they were fully clothed, because the way he was feeling right now, he might need to say a prayer that he didn't wake up inside her tomorrow like some kind of perverted rapist.

I'm going to hell.

He eased into a more comfortable position, careful not to disrupt her sleep, and let out a little sigh.

Alannah really was beautiful. And soft. She said he smelled good, but she smelled good, too. Trenton lifted a segment of her hair and sniffed. Oranges this time. He liked it as much as the honeysuckle.

She shifted and flung a leg over his, sending ripples of arousal coursing through his stomach. Through the little light that penetrated the room, he saw the hem of her dress had hiked up even further onto her hip.

He groaned, dragging his eyes away from her shapely thigh and the curve of her bottom. His pelvis tightened and he closed his eyes, while his body throbbed and pressure built in his groin. Silently, he begged sleep to overtake him.

His out-of-control libido eventually normalized, and Trenton threw his other arm across Alannah so she was wrapped securely in his embrace. This felt right. Comfortable. In a way he never experienced with other women.

Gradually he relaxed and his heart rate dropped. His eyelids became heavy and he closed them. And finally, thankfully, fell asleep.

Chapter Seventeen

She would never drink again. Never ever.

Alannah put a hand to her throbbing head and squinted in protest at the morning light. Fuzzy memories of the night before came back. She'd had more to drink than usual, and it had been a bad idea for sure. She vaguely remembered Trenton getting her into bed, during which she'd proceeded to molest him.

With a groan, she rolled her face into the pillow.

It smelled like him, a musky, manly scent that had her sighing internally and made her breasts tingle.

Then she remembered how she'd kissed him and begged him to stay the night with her. Could she be anymore pathetic? At least when she'd told him she loved him he probably didn't suspect the depth of emotion behind the words. Well, she hoped he didn't.

Alannah rolled out of his scent and onto her back, wishing she could escape the memory of her embarrassing behavior. Working her tongue around her dry, cottony mouth, she grimaced. *Gross.*

She floundered out of bed, arms flailing when a bout of dizziness made the room spin. She made her way across the floor, but minor nausea invaded her stomach and stopped her at the door of the bathroom. Clutching the doorframe, she steadied herself for what could have been long seconds or even a few minutes, before shuffling forward with careful, tentative steps. She turned on the light and winced, her head exploding into a crescendo of pain as if a percussionist had crashed his cymbals together inside her skull. She stumbled toward the sink and squinted at her reflection.

She looked like crap. Creases on her cheek. Smudged lipstick. Bloodshot eyes. Messy hair. Groaning again, Alannah hid her face with her hands. What must Trenton think of her?

After scrubbing her face clean of makeup, Alannah brushed her teeth and changed into a big T-shirt and black leggings. She popped some ibuprofen and made the trip down to the first floor to let Angel out the back to do her business.

Alannah was in the kitchen sipping ginger tea and nibbling saltine crackers, Angel eating near her slippered feet, when the doorbell rang. She frowned, wondering who in the world could be bothering her on a Sunday morning without calling first. She padded to the front door with the Yorkie trailing behind her.

She opened the door and frowned when she saw a Hispanic woman wearing medical scrubs and a pleasant smile, curly black hair held back from her face with a headband.

"Good morning, are you…" She consulted a clipboard. "Alannah Bailey?"

"Yes," Alannah answered cautiously.

"Good morning!" The young woman had an annoyingly chipper voice. "I'm Selena, with I.V. Nurse."

"I.V. Nurse? I'm not sick." Alannah looked past her to the unmarked white van in the driveway. "What is this about?"

The young woman smiled. "We're not dispatched to people who are sick. Our mobile service is for customers who suffer from…hangovers." She whispered the last word.

"How did you know—" The answer to the incomplete question came to her right away. Despite her relationship with the Johnsons and an intimate knowledge of their lifestyle, there were still moments when she was amazed at the services the rich procured, such as this one, which she'd never even heard of. But it smacked of being the kind of thing people of their ilk saw as a necessity. "Could you tell me who set up this appointment?" she asked, though she already knew the answer.

"Certainly. Mr. Trenton Johnson sent us." Selena didn't need to consult her clipboard to remember that name, and she said it with pride, honored to be dispatched at his request. "He reserved our top service for you."

Alannah folded her arms over her chest. "Is that right?"

"Yes. The call was made this morning. Give me a few minutes, and I'll go back to the van—"

"Excuse me, but what exactly is the service?" Curiosity got the best of her.

Selena launched into what sounded like standard company spiel in an upbeat, perky voice. "Dehydration causes some of the symptoms you're experiencing. Our specially formulated elixir hydrates you with a nutritious mixture of anti-inflammation and anti-nausea vitamins, minerals, and medicine. In no time at all, you'll feel much better."

"Really? Well, Selena, I'm sure your hangover remedy is wonderful, but I'll pass."

The young woman's confident smile faltered. "Ms. Bailey, Mr. Johnson has reserved our very best service for you, which includes a Vitamin B12 booster to help your energy levels. It's completely safe and the entire session only lasts about forty-five minutes."

"I'm not interested. And please pass on a message to Mr. Johnson. Tell him he no longer has to look out for me. I'm a grown woman and he can stop treating me like a child who needs to be protected." She made to slam the door, but then changed her mind and added, "And tell him to go to hell."

Then, with a tight smile, she slammed the door.

****

Trenton pulled his Range Rover to a squealing halt in front of Alannah's garage. The light at the second-floor window disappeared when the curtains in her bedroom closed abruptly. So she knew he had arrived.

He marched up to the front door and let himself in with his key. He almost tripped over Angel, who skidded toward him with the zest and speed of a much bigger dog. She barked and growled, ever protective of the homestead the way a lion was its pride. He stepped over his tiny black and brown adversary and stomped up the stairs. One day he was going to deal with that damn dog, but today was not the day. He had to deal with her hardheaded mistress first.

Alannah knew he was coming, so he flung open the door without knocking, and was unprepared for the sight before him. She stood in the middle of the room wearing a thin white robe. Her long hair had shrunk up into waves around her shoulders, and the room smelled of apple-scented shower gel from the open doorway of the bathroom.

His entire body tightened as his gaze encompassed her pert little breasts and full hips beneath the robe. Was she naked under there?

Alannah extended an open palm to him. "Give me my keys."

Trenton snapped out of the temporary hypnosis. "What for?"

"Because I want them."

"You going to give me mine?"

She marched over to her purse on the dresser, extracted the keys to the Maserati, the Range Rover, and his condo keycard, and held them out to him.

Trenton crossed his arms over his chest. He was not giving up her keys and had no intention of taking his. "Why didn't you use the I.V. Nurse?" The company had called to say Alannah canceled the service, and by the guarded tone of the conversation, he suspected his friend had been a difficult customer.

She tossed the keys onto the dresser. What was she so upset about? If anyone should be upset, it was him.

"I didn't need their services. I got some sleep and took a nice, warm shower and I feel perfectly fine. You wasted your time and money. Did they relay my message?"

"What message?"

"The one where I said you could go to hell? No, probably not. They wouldn't want to upset Mr. Trenton Johnson." She rolled her eyes.

"I don't know what your problem is, but your attitude is starting to piss me off. I've been with Cyrus all day entertaining clients. First at the country club, then lunch, then a tour of our offices, then dinner. You're not used to drinking that much, and since I was *working*, I wanted to make sure you were okay."

"I told you before, I don't need you to take care of me. I'm not a child, Trent." She slammed both hands on her hips. The motion made the robe gap open further, and involuntarily, his eyes lowered to her exposed chest. Less than an inch further to the right and he'd be able to see nipple.

"Would you put some clothes on?"

"I have clothes on."

"More clothes," he said between clenched teeth.

Alannah spread her arms wide. "This bothers you? You mean you notice what I have on?"

Trenton ground down on his teeth. "I noticed what you had on last night. I noticed you barely covered your ass."

"Well, I guess you were the only one, buddy. Because only one man approached me last night, and—"

"Somebody approached you?"

Her mouth fell open. "Unbelievable. There you go again. I *wanted* to be approached. Get that through your thick skull."

"By the losers at The Underground?"

"Oh, they're losers, now?"

"They're not good enough for you."

"I can make my own decisions."

"You need a nice guy. Someone who'll respect you and love you and treat you the way you deserve to be treated."

"I have a nice guy. Now I want a bad boy. Someone to screw my brains out."

Heat saturated Trenton's neck, and he took several labored breaths. "You really need to stop saying shit like that."

"Why? I mean it. The only problem is, no one ever notices me."

"You get noticed."

"Oh yeah? What about you, Trenton? Do you notice me?" Her eyes challenged him.

Trenton blinked. An invisible force vacuumed the air from the room. Tension tightened the muscles in his back and neck. He didn't know how to answer the question, wasn't sure if honesty would be appropriate. If she had any idea the dream he'd had, if she even suspected how sexually frustrated he'd been this morning when he woke up with her in his arms, she'd run far, far away.

"I threw myself at you last night," Alannah said.

"You didn't know what you were doing."

"I knew exactly what I was doing, and you were turned on. But you still treated me like a good friend. Like always."

Trenton laughed softly. "You have no fucking idea, do you?"

He hadn't slept well at all last night. Every time she moved, he jerked awake, practically climbing the walls with the need to fuck her. He'd woken up with a painful erection in the wee hours of the morning, torn because he needed to leave before he did something unseemly, but reluctant to go because he enjoyed how she felt in his arms.

Then he'd spent half the day fantasizing about her in that red dress and what her bottom would look like if he yanked the hem up over her hips and bent her across the bed. Or over the arm of the sofa. Frankly, anywhere he could get his hands on her hips and tilt them up for entry.

"Enlighten me," Alannah said. Her tongue swiped across her lips and she swallowed hard, as if mustering courage to continue. "You've never once made a pass at me, Trent."

"You want me to make a move on you? Is that what you're saying? You want me to *screw* you?"

Her breathing hitched. "Yes."

Her answer left him speechless. He hadn't truly expected that answer. "Do you have any idea what you're saying?" he growled.

"I know exactly what I'm saying."

One hand fisted at his side. "You know what I would do to you? What I want to do to you right now?"

"Why don't you tell me?" she said, voice wavering a little.

"I don't think you can handle a man with my appetite. I'm not one of your little boyfriends. I'm not Connor or TJ."

Alannah shifted her chin a fraction higher. "Prove it," she challenged.

Trenton stalked closer and noticed she held her breath. His gaze swept her face—the mutinous set to her pinkish mouth, the excitement of challenge in her eyes, the sprinkling of freckles on her makeup-free face. "You know what you're asking me?"

"I'm a big girl."

"This isn't a game, Lana."

"What are you afraid of, Trent? Scared I won't like it?"

That did it.

Trenton grabbed a handful of auburn waves and dragged her flush against his chest. Her eyes widened and lips parted on a rough exhale, as if she could no longer breathe through her nose. Tightening his hand in her hair, he tipped her head back so he could gaze straight down into her eyes.

"Nah. That's one thing I'm absolutely, positively not worried about."

He slammed his mouth onto hers and fed his hunger. Kissing her hard, he reacquainted his taste buds with the sweetness of her flavor. His probing tongue plundered her mouth and forced a whimper from her throat, and she sagged against him, grabbing his biceps.

She trembled, her entire body engulfed in shudders so profound he tore his mouth away and looked down at her with concern. He released her hair and cupped her shoulders. "Are you all right?"

Alannah nodded, breath quivering, eyes wide and expectant in her face. "I…" She rose up onto her toes, wrapped her arms around his neck, and pressed her body into his. "I've waited so long for this."

Her words sent shock waves through him. The burgeoning ache in his groin intensified and desire flooded his veins.

"I'm ready, Trent. I'm so ready." Then Alannah pulled his head down to hers.

Chapter Eighteen

Trenton's large hands seized her ribcage and Alannah tightened the grip around his corded neck, pulling herself higher to lay claim to his mouth. She sifted her tongue past his lips and opened for his sweet invasion. A breath-defying kiss ensued that had her curled over his strong forearm and grinding her hips into his. He demanded and she gave, her actions fueled by lust that had remained concealed for ages.

With an impatient motion, Trenton pushed the robe from her shoulders and uncovered her nakedness. He stopped long enough to stare at her with his jaw tight and his irises a deep, mossy green. She stood there, wondering what he thought. Wondering if she at least met the minimum standard of what he was accustomed to. But he didn't make a sound. He simply prodded her toward the bed until she fell backward into the pillows.

Alannah waited as he continued to watch her, his mouth set in a grim line. She fought the urge to cover her body as bashfulness and excitement wrestled for supremacy under his gaze. His eyes ran from her breasts, over the sweep of her hips, down to her toes. The longer he looked, the more labored his breathing became.

Nostrils flaring, Trenton brought his eyes back to hers and shook his head. "No fucking idea," he muttered.

A frisson of excitement scurried down her spine at the feral look in his eyes. Poised above her, with his body taut and rigid as if ready to pounce, he truly appeared to be like the mountain lion she'd compared him to. Lucky for her, this time she was the prey.

He lowered to the bed and clamped his wet mouth over a nipple. He sucked enthusiastically on her breast, making her moan and twist with pleasure. Arching her back, she symbolically pleaded for him to take more of her into his mouth—breathless as her trembling fingers tracked across the fine hairs of his head and her quivering thighs fell apart for him to do as he pleased.

Trenton continued to take his fill of each of her breasts, laboring over the aroused peaks with such diligence they could do nothing but stand at rigid attention under the intense ministrations of his masterful mouth. One of his hands went lower and covered her mound, and the unexpected touch made Alannah gasp and clutch his shoulders. The last of coherent thought dispersed like dust in the wind as he massaged her with a possessive touch that had her throbbing against his palm.

Unbearable sexual tension thrummed between her thighs, and she ached for release. She tried to trap his hand to get herself off, but Trenton popped up his head and looked into her eyes. "Not yet," he said, a devilish smile on his face.

Alannah whimpered her objection, almost ready to beg. But he ignored her protest and nudged her onto her stomach. Breathless with anticipation, she forced herself to lie still and was rewarded when he dropped moist kisses between her shoulder blades. Sucked the skin of her back. Licked the length of her arms. Everywhere he touched, pockets of flame erupted beneath her skin.

His tongue swirled in the shallow groove at the base of her spine before he lightly dragged it in a slow, torturous line along the crack of her ass. She moaned at the teasing caress and ragged, pleading mewls filled the pillow as her legs came a fraction apart.

"I see what you want." Trenton dragged her legs wider and licked the underside of her bottom. "You want this." The moist blade of his tongue swept the wet spot between her legs and air left her lungs in a rush as her eyes squinted closed. A deep, dark craving took hold of her, one that she desperately needed him to satisfy. Her body clenched and shoulders hunched, and she pushed back against him, hungering for the bold penetration of his tongue.

He laughed knowingly—a sound of complete control, rife with the confidence of a distinguished maestro in the midst of conducting his greatest symphony. Still he wasn't done, and continued down her thighs. He kissed the back of her knees and showered her with affection by nibbling on her calves and wringing pleasure from an unexpected place with strong caresses to her feet. She couldn't take much more of his teasing. Not when every nerve ending quivered with longing and every hair on her body seemed to stand on end.

The smack of his hand on her backside sent stinging pleasure to her core. His big hand squeezed her fleshy bottom and she lifted into the coarse handling. "Been wanting to do that," he said, a rough edge to his voice.

Alannah angled a look over her shoulder in time to see Trenton lever off the bed. He tossed off his shirt to reveal a smooth, muscular chest and abs that could make any professional athlete turn a vibrant shade of green from envy.

She twisted onto her back and pulled her bottom lip between her teeth, heart racing in anticipation. The tight cords of his arms bunched as he unzipped his pants, slowly, ever so slowly, as if putting on a show. He finally pushed them down with his boxer briefs and stood at the side of the bed, completely naked.

Allowed to examine him without restriction, Alannah rose up on her elbows and her gaze lowered to his hips. Her mouth fell open. She couldn't believe its size. The infamous Womb Beater surpassed her expectations.

It would never fit. He was too long and too wide.

The fear must have shown on her face, because Trenton rejoined her on the bed and spoke in a soothing voice. "It'll fit."

Panic set in, and Alannah's heart thumped at an alarming rate against her sternum. She scooted back from him. "I-I don't think it can. It's too big."

"Trust me."

"Trent, I—"

"Shh."

He lowered his naked body to hers and enveloped her in his warmth. With his body a cage over hers, he kissed her neck and chest, and spread her legs wide. Then his fingers found their way back to her sensitive core, and they tapped and stroked in the moisture discovered there.

"We'll get you good and wet," Trenton said, the gravelly words uttered against her neck.

Alannah kissed the corner of his mouth, relaxing into his touch and the rhythmic movement of his fingers. She ran her hands over his hard biceps, amazed at how a man so muscular could simultaneously be so soft. Desperately, she pressed open-mouthed kisses to his skin: along his Adam's apple, over his chest—anywhere within the limited scope of her mouth's reach.

Trenton inserted one, then two digits into her wet core, and she let out a loud gasp, overwhelmed with emotion as he curled his fingers against her G-spot and stroked her clit with his thumb. There was no way to withstand the force of his pleasure-giving touch. And when he sucked her nipple again, all Alannah could do was grab the muscles of his back and hold on tight until the tension broke.

The explosion ripped through her with the force of a hurricane. She whimpered and begged and pleaded, but Trenton didn't let up. His mouth remained fastened over one swollen, aching peak, and his fingers continued to pump between her legs as she rode out the climactic storm.

Trenton lifted his head as her body made one last shudder, and with his irises now the darkest green she'd ever seen them, he gazed into her eyes, and his lips twisted into a sexy grin. "We'll take it slow the first time. Until you get used to me." He licked her essence from his fingers and looked down between her legs. "Damn, you taste good. I'm coming back to that later."

The sensual threat made Alannah shiver with little aftershocks. But she didn't have much time to think, because Trenton slipped on a condom and then kneed her legs apart. Stretching her arms above her head, he locked her wrists in place with one hand. Now he had her how he wanted her. Dominated by his strength. Under his full control.

Alannah still worried about being able to accommodate him, but he slid in slowly, inch by powerful inch. Clearly considerate of her comfort, because she sensed him holding back. The tendons in his neck pressed into prominence, and he let out a low groan that came from deep in his chest.

He started to move—a slow, sliding thrust—and bent his head close to hers to whisper in her ear. He told her how sweet she was and how her wetness had him losing his mind. He told her how he couldn't wait to feel her coming all over him.

The words made her muscles relax, and she stretched to capacity, making it easier for her to accept his impressive manhood. She'd never felt this type of sensation before, this type of fullness in her life. His manly scent surrounded her, and his presence overwhelmed her. As if he wasn't only in her, but around her, and there was no way for her to evade a single part of his touch.

Trenton watched with fascination as renewed desire unfurled in Alannah's face—the pleasure-filled grimace, the closing of teeth around her lip. Every time he pushed down, she lifted her hips up to meet him. He glanced at the union of their bodies and watched how he sliced into her. The sight was the most erotic thing he had ever seen, and his muscles bunched tight under the ache of restraint.

He wanted to plow into her. He wanted to claim her with all his length. But he knew she wasn't ready and he'd promised to take it easy.

Pumping with a little more vigor, he bent his head to her pretty breasts. They were small and round, with tight little nipples that carried tints of rose and brown in equal measure. His tongue lashed across the tips and she twisted upward, her hips moving even faster as she easily matched his rhythm. He greedily sucked her into his mouth and tortured the tips of her breasts with his teeth. Enthusiastic cries filled his ears, and her writhing body stroked his ego.

As excitement mounted within him, Trenton didn't let up. One hand fisted on the pillow beside her head, keeping a determined rein on his climax until she achieved another one. The other hand lowered to behind a knee and lifted her leg around his waist so he could slide a little deeper.

Hands now free, Alannah sank her nails into his clenching buttocks. His control almost snapped right then, and he swore into her neck. Trenton drew deep breaths filled with the sweet aroma of her feminine scent. He traced the line of her arched throat with the tip of his tongue, certain no other woman's sweat had ever tasted as good.

His hips continued to move. Careful not to plunge too deep. Careful not to thrust too hard. Jaw tight, he simply held on, taking pleasure in her cries and reveling in the moist heat of her welcoming body.

A cry tore from Alannah's throat and her entire body tensed. Trenton slid his hand to her bottom and squeezed with his long fingers. She immediately exploded around him with climactic tremors more intense than the first time.

"T-Trent," she said, in a broken, feverish whisper that sheared shivers down his spine.

That was what finally pushed him to the brink. He abandoned himself to an intense orgasm that lashed ecstasy across his muscles and tightened his entire frame. The jarring climax pulsed through his blood as he careened over the edge, his body thrusting, his muscles aching, and his brain clouded by a fog of immeasurable sensual bliss.

****

In the dark bedroom, Alannah listened to Trenton wash up in the bathroom. She rolled onto her side, faced away from the door, and pulled the bed sheets up around her waist. She wondered with trepidation what would happen in the next few moments.

Was he a cuddler? If not, she'd be okay with that.

Would he leave when he came out? She'd be okay with that, too, she told herself, even though her stomach clenched in distress at the thought.

The bathroom door clicked open and a thin triangle of light slanted across the bottom of the bed before Trenton turned it out. Her throat closed as she listened to his quiet movements.

He slid onto the bed, and her heart thudded violently as he

shifted on the mattress. Her fingers tightened on the sheet as she waited.

Then he put his arms around her, pulled her in tight, and molded around her body.

Alannah relaxed into his embrace and breathed easier. This was more than she'd expected. She wanted to speak, wanted to ask the question that made her throat ache—*What now?* But fear kept her muzzled.

Her fantasy had come true, and she didn't want to spoil the moment with words.

So she clasped his hands in both of hers and closed her eyes to the tears of happiness that filled them almost to overflowing.

Chapter Nineteen

Waking up to Alannah's soft body was a nice surprise. After making love two more times, they'd fallen asleep spooning, and Trenton had slept the whole night through, in a deep, undisturbed slumber. He pressed his face into her auburn hair and inhaled the familiar scent. He was addicted to the citrusy fragrance now. Slowly, he felt himself growing hard and pressed his pelvis against her bottom. He hated to disturb her sleep, but he was horny again.

He kissed her neck and shoulders and eased a knee between her thighs. Moaning, she arched back against him.

"What are you doing?" Her sleepy morning voice was sexy, with a husky, throaty edge.

He responded by taking his hard penis in hand and positioning it between her legs. Then he rested his leg over hers for a tight fit. "You don't have to do a thing. Just let me…"

Groaning, Trenton kissed her bare shoulder. She was so soft and smelled so good, and he wanted to be close to her. As close as two people could get without penetration.

Alannah stretched and arched her back, pushing her body even tighter against him. Trenton covered one of her breasts, massaging the supple mass with gentle but firm strokes, and used his thumb to play with the tip. Rewarded with a puckered nipple against his palm, he grunted, sliding his length back and forth between her thighs.

"Wait," she whispered. She twisted in his arms and placed a featherlight kiss on his throat. "Get on your back."

Trenton followed the instruction and rolled onto his back. Through half-closed eyes he watched an impish smile slide across Alannah's lips as she took his stiff length in both hands and gently squeezed. He grimaced from the dart of pleasure, his body coming fully awake and excited at the prospect of further contact.

She stroked him into a more rigid form, the mischievous smile growing wider and extending into her hazel eyes. She kissed the rapidly beating pulse in the middle of his collarbone, and then moved her lips lower to suck his hard pecs.

He watched her through half-closed eyes as she kissed her way to his nipples and flicked them with her tongue. They turned into hard disks, surprising him, because he'd never really considered himself sensitive there before.

"Feels good, sweetheart," he murmured.

Alannah slid lower, the tangle of sheets and the warmth of skin-to-skin contact as she glided down his body turning him on even more. Trailing his fingers through her rumpled hair, he watched as she went lower and lower, past his diaphragm, over the taut muscles of his stomach, and lower still until his abdomen muscles tightened to the point of verging on pain.

With a sultry expression that took his breath away, she stretched her mouth over the broad tip of his shaft.

Trenton's toes clenched tight as she took him deeper, sucking and licking like she had a tasty Popsicle between her lips. The delicious suction of her mouth massaged the first half, while the lower half was caught in one of her hands. Her hand and mouth moved up and down on him in tandem, her tongue swirling and stroking the underside of his length like a pro.

Part of him loved it, and part of him hated that she was so good. It meant she'd done this before. Maybe even often. He thrust the disturbing thought away and concentrated on the visual before him. Of her pink mouth stretched wide over his shaft. How every now and again, the thick tip pushed out the side of her cheek—an erotic sight that would be emblazoned in his mind for a long time to come.

The pressure built in his balls, tightening until he was on the brink of erupting.

"I'm about to come, sweetheart," he groaned.

He had to warn her. Not every woman tolerated a man shooting into her mouth. But she didn't stop. He thought she hadn't heard him, because she continued in earnest. But then she gently massaged his balls and her gaze connected with his. She wanted him to let loose in her mouth.

Shit.

His head started swimming. "Lana…goddamn." His voice trembled, left hand curling into the sheets while his right hand cupped the back of her head.

She just kept going and going. Moaning, like she enjoyed it. Loved it, even. So enthusiastic he had to grit his teeth from the heightened excitement of watching her.

His last thought before he erupted into her mouth was that he never wanted anyone else to see her from this vantage point.

"Baby…I…*uh*!"

He grunted and his eyes closed tight to shut out the spinning room as he unleashed into her mouth. He pumped his hips, pushing as far between her lips as she allowed. His entire body shuddered. Vibrations extended from his center, out to every extremity, and folded his toes. He clutched a handful of her hair and held her head in place until he was limp from her having sucked every bit of his cum down her throat.

While he struggled to catch his breath, still in a state of awe, Alannah crawled up beside him and kissed the underside of his jaw. Then she covered half his body with hers and rested her head on his shoulder.

"You liked that?" she asked.

Liked was an understatement, and clearly she already knew the answer. She sounded mighty pleased with herself.

"It was good," were the only words Trenton could comfortably manage.

His voice had a little catch to it because he still hadn't caught his breath. If he kept talking he'd be gushing like a teenage boy who'd had his first nut. Mind a jumbled mess, he stared up at the ceiling.

He'd had plenty of head in his life—great head, fantastic head. There'd been women who'd deep-throated, women who were old pros, and he still had never had such a ridiculously good orgasm from oral sex. Never that intense. Never that explosive.

On top of him, Alannah's body had grown still and her breathing more even. She had fallen asleep again, and he lay there, loving the fact that she'd fallen asleep on him. The entire scene felt very comfortable, very…intimate.

The pulse in his neck beat a little faster. He had to get out of there. He needed breathing space and time to think.

Easing Alannah off him, he managed to escape her arms. She made a whimpering sound at the loss of contact, which he completely ignored.

"You're leaving?" she asked, in the same sleepy-sexy voice that sent shivers rippling down his spine.

"Yeah, gotta get going." He snatched up his clothes from the floor.

"Oh." Confusion clouded her voice.

She wondered what was going on, and since he didn't know himself, it didn't make sense to try to explain. He just knew he had to get out of there.

He dressed faster than he ever remembered dressing before, and that included the time in high school when he'd almost been busted in a girl's bedroom by her parents. It had to be a world record back then, and surely a new world record right now.

He put on his shoes standing up, resting one hand against the wall so he wouldn't have to sit on the bed and succumb to the temptation to roll over and pull her back into his arms.

At the door Trenton turned around, and Alannah was sitting up, clutching the blue-green sheet against her breasts. As if he didn't know what they looked like and hadn't had his mouth and hands all over them already, flicking the little hard nipples with his tongue and sucking until she squirmed restlessly beneath him.

She looked exactly the way he thought she would—lost,

confused, and still blinking sleep from her eyes. She brushed strands of hair off her forehead.

"Trent…?" she said, uncertainty in her voice.

"Thanks for…you know."

She flinched, and he knew it was the wrong thing to say, but she recovered quickly.

"S-sure." She swallowed, seeming to shrink a little in the big bed.

"I'll call you…um, later."

"Okay." She attempted a smile, but it looked forced, particularly when hitched to the pair of wounded eyes above.

He shut the door on his way out and ran down the stairs. Angel was in her little cage, and when she saw him, she charged out and barked fiercely—with more ferocity than she ever had before—as if she knew what he'd done. That he'd had his kicks and was running away.

He didn't threaten the dog this time. Angel had every right not to like him. He didn't like himself very much right now, either.

CHAPTER TWENTY

He never called.

Not the next day. Or the day after. Or the day after that.

Nothing. Not even a text.

For five solid days, Alannah didn't hear from Trenton. By the way he'd bolted from her bedroom, she'd expected this from him, but it didn't make the rejection any less painful.

She'd let her guard down, bared her soul, made love with him, and he'd run off. A routine night for him had been a momentous event for her.

She thought constantly about their lovemaking. The way he kissed away the delicious soreness of her backside after he'd given her a good spanking. Of him showering kisses on her back and neck as he slid in from behind. Of him tying her hands behind her back and sucking her nipples until she broke apart like shattered glass.

Alannah released an involuntary whimper and drew a trembling breath at the memories. She wasn't cold, but she sat on the sofa with her legs curled under her and a blanket thrown across her lap. It provided a modicum of the comfort she needed. So did the movie she had playing—one of her favorite foreign films, *The Thieves.*

Angel came prancing up to the sofa and stared up at her, whimpering, clearly sensing the somber mood and Alannah's pain.

She scooped up the dog, and the Yorkie licked her chin, whimpering some more.

"I'm okay," Alannah whispered to her little companion, rubbing the dog's head and around her ears. Tears brimmed and overflowed from her eyes. Sniffling, she quickly swiped them away and managed a quivering smile. "Trent will call." She tucked the dog under her chin. "He has to. He wouldn't…he wouldn't do me like that."

The dog whimpered again.

She and Trenton were friends, and he had to call eventually.

At least she'd done good so far. Though the temptation was great, she hadn't called him, and she resolved she'd leave it up to him to reach out.

****

Trenton entered Cyrus's office, his stomach such a tight batch of nerves that it actually hurt. When his brother had called to set up this meeting, he'd wanted to charge down here right away, but somehow he'd managed to rein in the impulse and wait the two hours until Cyrus could get rid of the guests in his office.

Cyrus handed Trenton a file. "That's everything on that Connor guy. Full name's Connor Aaron Bodell. Pretty boring stuff. He's never even had a parking ticket. Highlights are that he speaks several languages and lives with his mother. Apparently he moved here to take care of her. Been working at DymoGenesis for about eight months, and by all accounts he's doing a good job in the quality control department."

Cyrus stood at a corner of his massive desk and folded his arms, waiting as Trenton scanned the contents.

The enclosed photos showed a good-looking and clean-cut Caucasian male. He made regular donations to various charitable organizations. Fluent in Spanish, French, and Vietnamese. Vietnamese because he'd spent twenty months in Vietnam as part of a high-impact, targeted response team with the Peace Corps. The assignment had initially been for twelve months, but he signed up for an additional eight because he found the job particularly rewarding. Lots of volunteer work, including Meals on Wheels and the teen ministry at his church. Once saved a cat from a burning building—on the way to school, at the age of fourteen.

Trenton gripped the edge of the file. Somebody call the Catholic Church and nominate Connor Aaron Bodell for sainthood. Disgusted, he shut the folder.

"This can't be right. This is it? Everything?" The tightness in his stomach expanded and filled his chest.

"Everything. Looks like Alannah picked a great guy. This one's a keeper." Cyrus moved around the desk to sit in his chair. Clearly, he thought the conversation was over.

"Maybe it's the wrong guy," Trenton said.

Cyrus shook his head. "There isn't another Connor working at DymoGenesis. He's the right one."

"But this can't be everything," Trenton insisted, holding up the folder.

"You don't sound pleased."

"Maybe your guy made a mistake."

"He doesn't make mistakes."

"Maybe he did this time," Trenton snapped. "Isn't it possible he may have overlooked something? No way Connor is this damn perfect."

"His perfection is a problem?" Cyrus asked slowly.

Trenton took a deep breath. "Not a problem, per se."

"What is it exactly, per se?"

The sardonic note in Cyrus's voice registered. Trenton swiped a hand across his mouth and tempered his tone. "Never mind."

How could he possibly explain that he wanted—*needed*—Connor to be a loser or to secretly have a criminal past? Alannah knew all Trenton's secrets, his flaws, all his dirt, so he needed something he could use against Connor. Something that would make Trenton look like a viable choice.

"What's the real problem, Trent?" Cyrus asked quietly.

"Surprised, that's all."

"Surprised?" Cyrus cocked a brow. "Or disappointed?" His challenging gaze didn't stray from Trenton's face.

With a tight throat, Trenton managed to lie without lowering his gaze. "Surprised."

Then he marched out the door…knowing that he hadn't fooled Cyrus.

CHAPTER TWENTY-ONE

Avoiding the hired valets, Alannah parked her car on the grounds of the palatial estate belonging to Josh and Ingrid Baker. Their birthday celebration was an annual event and not to be missed.

The couple had married in their early twenties and remained two of the most entertaining of Trenton and Alannah's friends. Their parties were extravagant, legendary affairs that took months of planning for which they spared no expense—or at least Ingrid didn't.

Josh, a nerdy software developer with red hair and glasses, who'd rather sit in front of a computer than entertain a horde of guests, went along for the ride. He couldn't resist Ingrid and anything she requested.

Alannah didn't plan to stay at the party long. Only long enough to wish the couple a happy thirtieth birthday and see if Trenton was around. She just wanted to catch a glimpse of him, maybe say hi, and show him that she was doing fine even though he hadn't called.

With her heart fluttering lightly, Alannah exited the car and smoothed the ivory skirt of her cocktail dress. The top half was black with beaded detailing, and she'd played it safe tonight and worn three-inch heels. She nodded as she walked past the doorman, who swung open the door as she approached.

The grand foyer was a cavernous space where black and white

Italian tile covered the floor, and two staircases curved toward each other as they wound their way to the second level. A female server dressed in a white shirt and black slacks floated over to her, holding a tray of glasses filled with multicolored beverages. All of them looked yummy, garnished with pineapples, cherries, and olives.

"Ma'am, would you like a drink?" she asked.

"No, thank you." Since she was driving, Alannah had decided not to imbibe at all tonight. "Where are Ingrid and Josh?"

"The last time I saw them, they were in the kitchen. Do you know where that is?"

"Yes, I can find my way. Thanks."

Alannah spotted a silver box in the corner on a pedestal. Ingrid and Josh didn't accept gifts for their birthdays. Instead, they requested donations to their favorite charity, so she dropped the envelope-enclosed check she'd brought into the box and went in search of the hosts.

As the server had mentioned, she found them in the large, sparkling kitchen, surrounded by friends. Ingrid wore a sleeveless, cream-colored dress that brushed the tile when she moved. The round neckline showed a hint of café-au-lait breasts that looked suspiciously like they'd been contoured with makeup, and her short natural was colored a dark wine. In a word, Ingrid was striking.

Apparently, Alannah was striking as well. Ingrid did a double take when she saw her, and gasped.

"Alannah?" She placed her drink on the counter and floated over, mouth agape. "Turn around. Let me see you."

Alannah did a quick, self-conscious twirl. She'd grown comfortable with her new look and had forgotten there were people who hadn't seen her yet.

Ingrid cupped her own cheeks. "Oh my goodness, look at you. I barely recognized you. You're gorgeous!" she gushed.

Blushing, Alannah tucked her hair behind her ear. "Thanks." But she couldn't help but wonder, how bad had she looked before?

"Josh, look at her." Ingrid beckoned to her husband by waving her hand.

He frowned over at them from behind his spectacles.

"It's Alannah, honey," Ingrid said.

"Oh. Wow," Josh said, his gaze sweeping the length of Alannah's body.

"Hey, now," Ingrid chided her husband, laughing.

Other guests turned in their direction, which made Alannah even more self-conscious. She could feel the heat spreading downward into her neck, and she smiled politely and thanked the few people who immediately complimented her on the new look.

Ingrid put one had on her hip. "Trenton didn't even warn me about you."

"Oh, he's here already?" She kept her voice casual, but the pace of her heart increased.

Ingrid nodded. "Saw him earlier. Don't know where he is now, though. He could be anywhere. Maybe out at the gazebo? Somewhere holding court with his many admirers." Ingrid winked and nudged her.

Alannah smiled weakly, her stomach spiraling into a sickening plunge. Although Trenton had never left her stranded at a party, her attendance had never stopped him from getting a quickie from one or more of the female guests.

Ingrid had no concept of how much devastation her little joke caused. A joke that three months ago wouldn't have mattered as much, but after last weekend it cut with the sharpness of a dagger, and all the way to her heart.

"I'll see if I can find him," Alannah said.

"When you're done, come back. We need to talk about all this." Ingrid waved a manicured hand from the top of Alannah's head to her feet.

"I will."

Over the years, she'd attended many parties with Trenton. If for some reason they didn't go together and she arrived before he did, their friends always looked past her, searching for him. When they accepted she was alone, they'd ask if he was coming. When he did arrive, the excitement levels kicked up several notches. She'd seen him get this type of reception for years. Even during their school days, a party didn't start until he showed up, so she was certain that wherever he was, he'd be surrounded by people hanging on his every word.

Alannah started her search outside in the back, where guests congregated in the shadows, men and women flirting and chatting and whispering to each other. None of them were Trenton.

She continued to walk through the house, hovering in the doorways and searching the faces of the guests. In each room, she saw well-dressed men and women reclined in the plush chairs drinking and eating. Still no Trenton anywhere. She'd just about given up and was headed back to the kitchen when the bathroom door in the hallway opened.

Trenton came out, adjusting his clothes.

Despite herself, her heart leapt. She could barely contain her happiness at seeing him. "Trent." A small, hesitant smile hovered at the corners of her mouth. But he didn't look at all pleased to see her.

He froze, an expression of shock and guilt filling his face. At first she thought the guilt was because he hadn't reached out to her since they'd had sex, and she opened her mouth to tell him it was okay. That she forgave him. But movement in the bathroom caught her eye, and what she saw inside dealt her heart a crushing blow. He hadn't been alone in there.

As the door eased closed, she caught a glimpse of Beth, the girl he'd taken to Las Vegas, applying a fresh coat of lipstick to puckered lips. Her long weave of black, shiny curls cascaded down her back to her waistline, and the skimpy black tube dress she wore emphasized every curve of her voluptuous body.

Alannah couldn't move. Couldn't speak. Pain seized her vocal cords and the walls in the small space they occupied seemed to close in and make it hard to breathe.

"Lana."

Slowly, her gaze drifted to Trenton. Contrition filled his eyes, but the moment wasn't over. Beth exited the bathroom and almost ran into him because he was still standing in the doorway.

"Oh, excuse me." She looked from one to the other and smiled. "See you later, Trent." She snapped her clutch closed and blew him a kiss. Then she walked away, clearly adding an extra switch to her hips for his benefit.

"Lana, I can explain—"

"You *pig.*"

She wouldn't cry. She *would not cry.*

Alannah stormed down the hallway and rushed toward the door.

"Lana, wait. Please."

She pushed out of the door and into the night, taking firm, hard steps that propelled her out to the yard.

"Good night, ma'am," the doorman called.

A horrible, twisted joke, because there was absolutely nothing good about the night now. She shouldn't have come. She'd just wanted to see him but hadn't expected this. She knew his MO better than anyone else and had seen him break hearts all his life. Why did she think he'd treat her any differently?

"It didn't mean anything. I was just…"

Almost to the car, Alannah swung around on him. "You were just what? Say it."

He remained silent.

"Say it."

"I'm not going to say that."

"Say it. Be man enough to say what you were doing."

He looked away from her, his face hidden in the shadows cast by the ground lights against the bushes and trees. "It was nothing, Lana," he said quietly. "I let her blow me, that's all. It's not a big deal. I just needed to get the edge off, but I didn't even come."

"You didn't come. Poor baby. You really think that makes it okay?" she asked in a tremulous whisper. "You know what, I don't care what you do. It's your penis. Do whatever you want with it. Stick it in the mouth of anybody you want." Her chest hurt, a deep, ingrained ache she knew wouldn't leave anytime soon. He stayed quiet, so she kept talking. "If you want to get your dick sucked by Betty Blowjob and all her pals, that's up to you. I really don't care."

Betty Blowjob. She didn't even know where that ridiculous name had come from.

Trenton finally looked at her, and in the dim light she saw concern in the wrinkling of his brow and the tight set of his jaw. "I don't care about a blowjob—"

"No? You sure don't act like it."

"Baby—"

"No!" She shoved a finger in his face. "Don't you call me baby. Don't you dare!" Her voice went up ten octaves. The scenery grew hazy as she teared up. Heat filled her face and she knew her skin was a mottled red from the combination of anger and trying not to cry. "I'm not one of your jump-offs."

"I never said you were." He looked and sounded very sorry.

"I'm better than that." Her voice cracked. "You know I am." She had to be. They'd known each other for twenty-two years. She *had* to mean more to him than just sex.

"Alannah, shit." He clutched his head. "I messed up. Don't go. Let's go somewhere and talk."

"I do not want to talk to you. I do not want to see you."

She swirled away from him again and continued the march to her Lexus. The car he had bought, which made her want to cry even more.

"Wait. Please, Alannah, don't go. Talk to me."

He caught her arm, but she yanked away and shoved him. He hardly moved, which made her even angrier. She wanted to push him so hard he fell to the ground. She wanted to hurt him, the way he'd hurt her. He needed to suffer.

Her fingers curled into angry fists. "I hate you, Trenton," she said in a broken voice. He flinched, as if she'd dealt him a physical blow. She shook with the anger and pain that filled her, and tears welled up and fell onto her cheeks. She didn't care anymore if he saw. He needed to see that he'd done a horrible, terrible thing. "I *hate* you."

Slowly, she backed away. He didn't follow this time, but he continued to stare at her. The further away she backed, the harder it was to see his face against the backdrop of lights.

Alannah swiped a hand across her cheeks and spun toward the car. She unlocked it, jumped in, and started the engine right away. Sniffling, she slammed the accelerator and drove off, not looking back at him. She turned a hard right out of the iron gates and onto the main road, but didn't get far. The tears streaming down her cheeks made it difficult to see, so she had to pull over onto the shoulder.

She shoved the car into park and switched on the hazard lights. Sobbing, she hugged the steering wheel and pressed her wet cheeks against her arms. The only explanation for such gut-wrenching pain was that her heart must have been torn completely in two.

Her shoulders heaved from the severity of her sobs. And Alannah cried…and cried…and cried.

CHAPTER TWENTY-TWO

"Are we boring you?"

Cyrus's voice pulled Trenton into the present.

"What?" he said.

"Are we boring you?" Cyrus asked again.

Ivy, across from him, arched a brow. They were seated in the small conference room adjacent to Cyrus's office.

"No, you're not boring me," Trenton said.

"Then please give me the most recent reports on the racial demographics of our customers. I'm particularly interested in seeing if the target marketing to the Latino community has expanded penetration in specific pockets around the country." Cyrus held out his hand.

Trenton shuffled through the stack of papers in front of him. He saw Ivy's data on the restaurant group and the figures Cyrus had disbursed about the overall health of the company.

"I must have left them in my office," he mumbled. He could feel his cheeks turning red. Normally, he was better prepared than this. From the corner of his eye, he saw Cyrus and Ivy look at each other.

"In that case, there's nothing further to discuss," Cyrus said, sounding annoyed. "Our meeting is adjourned."

The three of them rose from the chairs and Trenton filed out behind his siblings. Halfway across the floor of Cyrus's office, he realized he'd left his siblings' reports in the small conference room. No point in going back and highlighting his absentmindedness. It was better to leave, but luck was not with him.

"Hang on a minute, Trent," Cyrus said.

He groaned inwardly. Ivy sent a look of pity over her shoulder before she exited.

Taking a deep breath, Trenton turned to face his brother, now standing behind his immense desk, the Seattle skyline spread out like a giant photo behind his back.

"What's going on?" Cyrus asked.

Trenton affected a frown of confusion. "Nothing. I'm human and sometimes I make mistakes. I'm having a bad day, that's all."

"You're having a bad week." Cyrus dropped the stack of reports on his desk.

Trenton stiffened. "What?"

"You're having a bad week."

"I heard you the first time," Trenton bit out.

"Then why did you ask me what I said?"

"I'm not in the mood for this." He didn't want to be picked apart. "I've got a lot on my mind, okay?"

They stared at each other in silence.

"Have a seat." Cyrus waved toward one of the guest chairs in front of him. Trenton didn't move. "*Have a seat.*"

Reluctantly, Trenton trudged over to the chair and sat down. He gritted his teeth and prepared for the berating his brother was about to dish out.

Cyrus sank into his executive chair and crossed his legs. "You slept with her."

Startled, Trenton's head reared back. "What are you talking about?"

"Don't play dumb. You slept with Alannah, and I know because she abruptly canceled on our Fourth of July lake party. I can't remember the last time Alannah didn't go out on the boat with us for the Fourth. She canceled *by text,* to Mother of all people, and without explanation, which is very unlike her. It was obvious when you showed up you had no idea she wouldn't be there, and it's also very obvious how screwed up in the head you are." He let his observations sink in before he continued. "I told you not to sleep with her. You did it anyway, and now everything's a mess."

Trenton fisted his hands on the arms of the chair. "Goddammit, Cyrus, does it really make you feel good to say 'I told you so' right now?"

"Believe me, I wish I were wrong. You have no idea what a burden it is being right all the time."

"Unbelievable." When one corner of Cyrus's mouth pulled a fraction higher, Trenton relaxed. "You're such an asshole."

The smile stretched to the other side of Cyrus's mouth. "What happened?"

Trenton stood from the chair, suddenly feeling restless. "Like you said, I slept with her, and now I'm all screwed up." He ran both hands over his head and down his face. "I don't know whether I'm coming or going." It took a lot to admit that. He walked back and forth across the carpet. Cyrus didn't say a word, just watched his movements.

Trenton needed to fill the void of silence, so he kept talking. "You want to know the best part?" He came closer and rested his hand on his brother's desk, careful not to disturb the meticulously laid out pens along the edge. "She was the best sex I ever had. I've slept with countless women, but Lana…she was the best I ever had. Can you believe it? You'd think I never had any ass before." Trenton pushed away from his brother's desk. "What's wrong with me?"

"I know that was a rhetorical question, but I have an answer. You're in love with—"

Trenton reared back even further. "No way. No fucking way. In love? What am I, a chick who catches feelings after some good dick? No. Hell no." He shook his head to emphasize the point.

"I'm not saying you fell in love with her because of great sex. I'm saying you—"

"Shut up, Cyrus." He pointed a finger at his brother. "You don't know what you're talking about. I know you think you know everything and think you're always right, but this time you're dead wrong."

Cyrus lifted his hands in mock surrender. "Okay, I'm not going to push it, because you're obviously not ready to accept the truth."

"No, you're wrong."

"Okay, whatever. But you still have a problem, and it's causing you to be distracted."

Trenton sighed heavily. "Yeah. The problem is, she won't talk to me." She wouldn't even return his texts. He went by her house once and rang the doorbell. He heard Angel barking like crazy on the inside, but Alannah never came to door. When he tried to use his key, he couldn't get in. She'd changed the locks.

"Why won't she talk to you?"

"I did something stupid." Cyrus raised a brow, as if to silently say that was not unusual. Trenton rolled his eyes at his brother's judgment and kept talking. "I'm not telling you what I did, but I have to figure out how to get through to her. She's special to me, and I just…I want…" He swallowed. "I want her back."

He didn't even know why he'd behaved the way he did—why he'd run, why he'd hooked up with Beth. All he did know was that he couldn't lose Alannah. She'd been such an important part of his life for so long, he couldn't imagine never having that camaraderie again. He'd never had it with anyone else. Didn't want it with anyone else.

"You want her back on your terms," Cyrus said.

"What's that supposed to mean?'

"You say she's special, but I'm willing to bet you treated her like every other woman you've ever slept with."

He'd been having sex since he was thirteen years old. How was he supposed to reverse that many years of the same behavior?

Cyrus went into lecture mode. "You know her, probably better than anyone else. Think about your relationship. Think of it as…a sales and marketing project. How do you normally tackle issues regarding new demographics or increasing sales? You look at the research, and you have plenty of it. You have over twenty years of information and data you could mine to figure out how to get through to her. Use what you know. That's how you'll get her back. That's how you'll convince her that she's special to you."

Trenton nodded and saw the wisdom in his brother's words. "You're right." He grinned, the heavy load of loss lifting somewhat from his shoulders. "You're absolutely right." Excited, he rushed toward the door, energized by the prospect of winning Alannah over. He rubbed his hands together, his mind turning over the possibilities. He'd start slow, with something simple.

Cyrus called out to him, and Trenton paused with his hand on the door. "I know, I know, I'll get those reports to you." Cyrus may have been helping him with a personal issue, but the bottom line was, they had a business to run.

He opened the door but paused to look over his shoulder. His brother was already back to work, writing notes in the pad on his desk. The times Trenton saw him truly relax were with his wife, Daniella. They'd recently reconciled after a long estrangement and were expecting their first child. The entire family agreed that she was good for him. She worked hard, too, but she made Cyrus slow down. With a baby on the way, he imagined his brother would slow down even more. It was no secret how much he looked forward to fatherhood, and Trenton was pretty sure he'd be good at it, like he was everything else.

"Hey, Cyrus." His brother looked up, a frown on his forehead from being in deep thought. "Thanks."

Cyrus waved his hand dismissively and returned his attention to his notes. Trenton smiled and closed the door on his way out.

Chapter Twenty-three

Trenton slid in beside a royal-blue hybrid SUV in Alannah's driveway.

Not recognizing the vehicle, he frowned and turned off the Range Rover's engine. He sat in the darkness, staring at the light behind the drawn drapes of the living room window on the first floor. Maybe he should leave and come back another time.

But almost as soon as he had the thought, he changed his mind. He'd been determined to see her, even if it meant waiting out front all night until she let him in. So he'd go through with what he had planned. His heartfelt apology should be even more impactful when done in front of an audience, complete with the bouquet of pink and white carnations he'd picked up at a florist.

Taking a deep breath, he exited the SUV and walked up to the door. He shifted the bouquet to the left hand, slid one of his winning smiles into place, and rang the doorbell.

Seconds later, the door swung open and the smile died on his face. A man he'd never seen before, in the flesh at least, stood in the living room—Caucasian, dirty blond hair, and a surprised expression on his face. Mr. Perfect, Connor Aaron Bodell.

"Hi. You're Trenton Johnson."

Being from a high-profile family, he was accustomed to people knowing who he was, but this greeting irritated him. Mainly because Connor was on the inside while Trenton was stuck on the outside.

Connor extended his hand. "I've heard a lot about you."

Trenton took his hand and gave it a few hard pumps. "I haven't heard that much about you."

"Well, Alannah and I haven't been dating long." He looked at the flowers and a frown arrowed down between his brows.

"Who's at the—" Alannah had come from the kitchen and stopped talking the minute she saw him. Her features settled into a scowl. "What are you doing here?"

Trenton's gaze passed over the tight jeans, which fit so close they could have been tattooed on her body. The black top she wore wasn't much better, clinging to her small bust and narrow torso. His mouth tightened. "Don't you look nice," he said.

Her chin jutted out. "Thank you."

"What's *he* doing here?"

Her eyes passed over the flowers in his hand, but her expression didn't change. "He's an invited guest. You're not."

"I've never needed an invitation before." Trenton barged in, forcing Saint Connor to step out of the way.

Trenton and Alannah stared at each other across the living room. Behind him, he heard the door close, and on the television a *French* film was playing. Of course.

"We need to talk," Trenton said.

"Now is not a good time."

"Now is the only time I'm available."

Alannah let out an exasperated sigh and rolled her eyes. "Excuse me, Connor. We'll be able to get back to our evening as soon as I get through with this inconvenient interruption." She shot a dark look at Trenton and then stalked toward the kitchen.

Trenton cast a glance over his shoulder at Connor, now seated on the sofa and watching him with a curious expression.

He went into the kitchen and found Alannah standing with crossed arms in the middle of the floor.

"You should have called first," she said in an angry whisper.

"Why?"

"Obviously because I have company."

"Why is he here?"

"What do you want?"

"So you're not going to answer my question?"

"I don't owe you an explanation. We're both free agents, able to do whatever we want with whomever we want."

Not liking that answer at all, he gritted his teeth. "I bought these for you." He extended the flowers to her.

"You actually went to a store and picked those out?" she asked, not moving to accept his gift.

"Yes."

"You mean you didn't get Diana to do it for you?"

"I said *I* picked them out. I went to the florist and specifically asked for carnations because I know they're your favorite."

Her face remained impassive. "You wasted your time."

Trenton set the flowers on the bar and took a deep breath. "You're not going to make this easy for me, are you?"

"I don't know what you want, Trent. I didn't hear from you for an entire week, and then when I do see you, you're doing the same thing you always do—hooking up. Nothing changed. Tell me what you want so I can get back to my company."

"You think I'm going to leave you here with him, with you dressed like that?" He scanned her body, even more annoyed when he noted once again how tight the jeans and shirt were. "You must be out of your goddamn mind."

"There's nothing wrong with the way I'm dressed."

"Everything is wrong with the way you're dressed," he fired back.

"If it bothers you so much, get out."

"*I just said*, I'm not leaving you here alone with him."

"You don't have a choice."

"Actually, I do. *He's* getting out of here."

"No, you are. You can't throw him out. I'm throwing you out."

"Wrong. Trust me, he's leaving, and he's leaving all on his own. Watch."

Trenton strutted back to the living room and went to stand over

Connor on the sofa. He smiled when the other man looked up at him. "It's time for you to go."

"Go? I don't understand—"

"Stop it, Trent!" Alannah said behind him.

"Alannah and I need privacy. Two's company, three's a crowd and all that."

"What's going on?" Connor looked around Trenton to Alannah.

"No, look at me," Trenton said, speaking in a calm voice. "I'm trying to be nice, but pretty soon I won't be nice anymore. So I'm asking you again, please leave. Now."

"Stop trying to intimidate him."

"I'm not trying to intimidate him," Trenton said, watching Connor's expression shift from confusion into quiet alarm.

"If you lay a hand on him…"

"I won't do anything to him—personally. I can pay someone to do that for me. Someone who can make it look like an accident."

"Trent!"

Connor jumped to his feet. "I think you're right. I better go."

"Good idea," Trenton said.

Connor edged around Trenton and rushed to the front door. Alannah hurried after him, and Trenton flexed his fingers so as not to yank her back.

She placed a hand on Connor's arm. "You don't have to leave."

"It's best that I do." He eyed Trenton warily. "You're a wonderful woman, Alannah, and I was looking forward to getting to know you better. But you and"—his gaze moved to Trenton again but jumped away—"you and your friend need to figure out what you're doing."

"He's bluffing," Alannah said.

"No, I'm not," Trenton interjected.

She glowered at him, but her attention returned to Connor when he took her hand. "Maybe it wasn't meant to be. Take care." He patted her hand and left.

Quiet descended on the room. Even Angel didn't make a sound. She watched from the safety of the cage's interior as the night's events unfolded.

Alannah didn't say a word and simply marched past Trenton, as if he wasn't even there.

"Alannah." He caught her by the arm and she yanked away.

"Get out."

He'd never heard her voice so low and filled with fury. Duplicate circles of red suffused her cheeks, and her eyes spat green and brown flames.

"I have something to say."

"I don't want to hear it." She pointed to the door. "Go. Now. You're not welcome here."

"And he was? Why the hell is he welcomed and not me?"

She stared at him and refused to answer.

Trenton walked closer. "I asked you a question."

"I don't have to answer you."

"Why was he here? Why are you dressed like that?"

"I didn't do anything wrong. You can't make me feel guilty."

"Feel guilty about what? Be woman enough to say it," he said, repeating a variation of the same words she'd thrown at him outside Ingrid and Josh's home.

"You want me to tell you?"

"That's what I said."

"Fine. I wanted to sleep with him…to…"

Trenton listened, jaw aching from clenching his teeth so hard. "To hurt me," he finished for her.

She bit the inside of her bottom lip, the way she always did whenever she fought back her emotions. After a couple of blinks, she responded in a quiet voice, "Yes."

"That's not like you. That's not the kind of thing the Alannah I know would do."

"I'm not the Alannah you knew."

"You're the same Alannah I've always known. If you'd had sex with him, you would have hated yourself for using him."

"Nice try, Trent, but I'm sure I would have been fine." She cocked a brow at him. "I need to have my needs met, too. Maybe I wanted someone to go down on me tonight. You know, just to take the edge off." Her eyes challenged him.

Trenton felt bile rise in his stomach, nauseated by the thought of another man putting his head between her legs. Kissing her, tasting her, owning her with his mouth. "That is *not* okay." Her eyes widened. He stepped closer and towered over her, forcing her to tilt her head back to look him in the eye. "No other man is allowed to do anything to you—touch you, kiss you, or go down on you."

"You're such a hypocrite." Pain shone through the anger in her eyes.

His gut burned with shame. "I'm sorry about the thing with Beth. I feel like shit."

"Good, because that was a shitty thing to do." She averted her face from him, but not before he caught a glimpse of her pained expression. "How could you…do that?" she asked in a tremulous voice.

The sound of her hurting gutted him.

Her arms closed over her midsection in a protective fold. "I know we never said…I mean…I just thought…"

Trenton reached for her and then withdrew, unsure if she'd pull away from his touch. "I messed up."

"Yes, you did." She looked up at him, eyes laden with vulnerability. "You hurt me. Every other time I've been hurt, I could come to you. I could cry on your shoulder, but *you* were the one who hurt me."

"Alannah, sweetheart…"

"You didn't even call after. You acted like I didn't matter to you." Her voice thickened at the end.

"Didn't matter?" Trenton expelled a deep breath. "You know you matter, you've always mattered, but I could control the situation. Now that you've changed I feel you slipping away from me. You've changed your hair, you've changed your clothes. You don't return my calls. You're dating a man who's so perfect he makes me *sick*." He stared down into her shocked face. "You matter. You matter too much. Goddammit, Alannah, you matter so much that I *need* you. Like air. Like water. Like food. I—" He took a deep breath, struggling to articulate everything he felt inside. Finally, he clenched his fists and said with resignation the words he'd fought to acknowledge for far too long. "I love you."

Her mouth fell open.

"I do." He stepped close and cradled her face in his hands. Her eyes held a combination of wonder and confusion. "I fucking love you. Everything you do lately has been driving me out of my mind, and it's because I love you. Connor can't have you. I'll camp outside your house every night if I have to. If he tries to weasel his way back into your life, I'll have somebody break both of his legs until he wises up and leaves you alone."

Her eyes widened. "You can't—"

"I'm serious. I'll do it. I'll do whatever it takes, because I love you. I. Love. You."

Her gaze lowered to his mouth, anticipating, and his head swooped down to give her exactly what she expected. Fisting his hand in her hair, Trenton pulled her in tight and lowered his lips to hers in a kiss that made his heart skip a beat. As her arms locked around his neck, he kissed her with rising passion, a man who understood the value of the prize he had and couldn't afford to let anyone take it away from him.

"Baby," he murmured.

She placed little pecks against his mouth, nipping at the corners with her lips and teeth. The teasing ignited hunger in his blood. He had to make love to her. They'd been apart for too long.

Growling low in his throat, Trenton tossed Alannah over his shoulder like a caveman and raced up the staircase. He kicked open the door of her bedroom so hard it bounced back from the inside wall, but he'd already taken long strides to the bed and tossed her onto it.

Moving quickly, he dragged her pants and underwear over her hips and dropped them to the carpet. Then he stood back and just stared at her, feasting his eyes on her nakedness. His gaze drank in the bare legs, the trimmed mound, and the softness of her flat belly.

She covered her most intimate place with trembling fingers in a tentative display of modesty. But Trenton brushed her hands away and licked his lips, contemplating how she'd taste when he put his mouth on her again.

He grabbed a pillow and put it under her bottom, tilting her hips up to just the right angle.

"Still mine?" he asked, placing a possessive hand over her heated flesh and stroking his digits through the slick moisture he found.

"Yes," she said breathlessly, writhing under his touch.

"I want to hear you say it."

"Yes, it's yours. *I'm* yours."

He grabbed her calves and pushed her knees back to her chest, keeping her legs wide. She twisted in anticipation, but he held her fast.

"Nobody gets to go down on you but me."

He lowered his head between her legs and used gentle flicks to taste the moisture between them.

"Trent." His name trembled on the tip of her tongue, and the sound sent shivers shimmying down his spine.

An all-consuming need to drive her out of her mind, to turn her inside out, consumed him. He ravaged her with his mouth, groaning at the delicious taste of her juices as he circled her drenched clit and plucked at the sensitized folds.

Her hands found their way beneath her black top and she fingered her nipples, eyes closed, quietly chanting his name. Attuned to her body, he monitored each reaction—how her hips moved when he deepened the intensity of each stroke, how the decibels of each moan increased with the speed of every swipe.

His reward was a gasping cry when she climaxed hard in a display of shakes that gave his ego a hefty stroke and left him with a self-satisfied smirk on his face for a job well done.

Alannah lay there, moaning, saturated with pleasure, when he informed her, "I'm just getting started."

With his help, she wriggled out of her top, which he then tossed to the floor with her other clothes. He shrugged off his shirt and then his pants followed suit. Quickly he donned a condom and came down on top of her. He tasted her lips again, their mouths meshing together in a soul-searing kiss.

Turning her onto her side so she faced away from him, Trenton breathed into her ear, "Guess what else?"

"What?"

"You getting all this dick tonight."

Alannah inhaled sharply, closing her eyes as if the very thought was too much to contemplate.

"Think you can take it?" Trenton asked.

"Yes," she said softly.

He spread his fingers over the flat line of her belly and slid down to the damp curls below. "Let me hear you say it, sweetheart."

"I'm taking all this dick."

She reached back and fondled him, stroking his length until he groaned into her neck. He pressed against the cushion of her butt and gripped her hips with a firm hand. "That's right," he said, voice strained and thready as he readied for entry.

Broken breaths emitted from her throat as he turned her onto her stomach and entered her from behind. He started slowly, taking the sounds of pleasure as encouragement to slide deeper. His hands canted her hips higher, his own breathing a fractured and labored sound.

"You okay, sweetheart?"

"Yes," she panted, pushing back, urging him to fulfill his promise.

That was all the encouragement Trenton needed. He thrust his hips and surged inside of her.

Alannah cried out and curled her fingers into the sheets. Her entire being focused on the spot between her legs, where Trenton's thrusting motion grew more and more urgent. She bounced her hips higher, every muscle concentrated on accommodating him.

He set his mouth to her ear. "That's it. It's all yours, sweetheart. Take all this dick."

His mouth was a hot suction on her back. His big hands were hot clamps that held her fast so he could plant his body deeper. Excruciating pleasure spiraled through her blood and eclipsed the discomfort she initially experienced.

"Still with me, baby?"

"Yesss."

"Good. Cause I want you to love it, sweetheart." He spoke

softly, his lips pressed to the sensitive groove behind her ear. "I want you to love this dick."

Alannah gasped, body shivering at his erotic request. Pleasure and pain comingled, and her body creamed around him, making it easier for him to slide even deeper. She'd never known this type of sensation, such an unprecedented fullness that left her gasping for air.

Trenton muttered something incoherent and pumped his hips even harder. Alannah bit down on her lip and balled her hands on the pillows, lowering her shoulders and readying for the climax already winding its way through her loins. When her body exploded, she cried out in a loud voice and arched her back at a very sharp angle. Seconds later, using long, powerful strokes, Trenton ejaculated with a guttural groan and swore into her neck.

Collapsing beside her, Trenton dragged Alannah into his arms. His shallow breaths disturbed her tangled hair, and his arm rested loosely around her waist.

"Trent," she whispered, reaching back for him. She curled her arm around his neck.

"I'm right here, Lana." He shifted a muscular thigh over hers and pressed his lips to her shoulder. "I'm right here."

CHAPTER TWENTY-FOUR

Alannah curled up against Trenton, fitting to his body like a soft, malleable compound.

"Those jeans you had on tonight." He sighed. "You're gonna have me getting in all kinds of fights dressing the way you do."

"That would not be wise. You'll be hit with a bunch of lawsuits."

"Stop dressing that way, then."

"Behave. They're just clothes."

"To you, they're just clothes. To a man, they're the gateway to a vivid imagination." He idly ran his fingers up and down the arm she had thrown across his torso. "Definitely can't let Gavin ever see you in those jeans or anything else remotely tight-fitting." His older brother was off in South America, living the daredevil life he loved so much.

"Why?"

"He said something about you at Ivy and Lucas's engagement party."

"What did he say?"

"He paid you a compliment. I can't really remember what he said."

She tweaked his nipple and he flinched, pretending that it hurt. "Tell me what he said, or next time I'll do it harder."

"He said he always thought you were kind of cute. Damn."

"Gavin thinks I'm cute?" She rose up on an elbow. "Even with the way I used to dress?"

"Don't sound so happy."

"I'm not."

"Why're you smiling, then?"

"Am I?" She bit down on her lip.

"Yes," Trenton said, scowling.

"I'm surprised."

"That's not a surprised face, that's a happy face."

"Okay, fine, I'm flattered."

"I'm definitely keeping you two apart," he muttered.

She settled against his shoulder again. "Hee-hee, Gavin thinks I'm hot."

"Nobody said anything about you being hot. Just because you have a luscious ass, tasty nipples, and you're beautiful inside and out, doesn't make you hot."

Alannah shifted her gaze up so she could see his face, and he looked down at her. A sweet smile came across her face. "Thank you," she said.

Trenton squeezed her tighter and brushed his thumb across her bottom lip. "It's true. You're beautiful, Alannah. I can't believe you ever doubted that." He briefly pressed his mouth to hers and then settled back against the pillows.

Alannah laced her fingers between his. "You weren't very nice to Connor. I can't believe you made him leave."

"Fuck him."

"Trent, I have to face him at work."

"So what? You have nothing to be embarrassed about. He's the one who should be embarrassed. He let another man intimidate him into leaving a woman he's interested in."

"You really believe he was wrong for letting that happen, don't you?"

"Absolutely."

"You *threatened* him."

"Your point is…?"

She huffed. "Never mind."

"What?" Trenton watched her pluck a loose thread in the sheet.

"I don't have anything else to say."

"Not true. You want to say something else."

She ran a fingertip along the circumference of the sun on his chest. "Why do you dislike Connor so much? He's a really nice guy, and he never did anything to you."

"Wrong. He did do something to me. Or he almost did."

"When?" She lifted her head off his shoulder. "You don't even know him."

Trenton swung his head in her direction and his gaze held hers. "Connor did the worst thing possible. He almost came between us. He and I will never be friends." He spoke in an austere, succinct manner, to make sure she understood he meant every word.

Alannah rested her head back on his shoulder. "So you don't want me to see Connor. Is it just him?"

"I don't want you seeing anybody else but me."

She didn't respond for a full minute, but he felt the stillness in her body. "And what are you going to do?" she asked quietly.

"I'm not seeing anybody else either."

"Not even Beth?"

Trenton tipped her chin up with his finger, forcing her to look him in the eye. "Beth who?"

****

They went to a late dinner at The Best Thai Restaurant, and after they arrived back at Alannah's townhouse, Trenton walked in with her. Reluctant to leave, he held her in the middle of the living room, one hand on each butt cheek, their foreheads together.

"I need to go," he said.

Alannah groaned. "No." She tightened her arms around the trunk of his body and pressed her cheek against his chest.

"Yes." He patted her bottom. "I'm going to Mother's tomorrow for dinner. You coming?"

"I can," she said into his shirt, still sounding unhappy and holding him just as tightly.

"You want me to pick you up?"

"Okay."

He brushed his lips across her brow and then walked to the door, pulling her behind him. He turned at the door. "You're good, right?"

"Yes." She nodded.

"I took care of your needs tonight? You're straight? You no longer need to get the edge off?"

She blushed. "No, I'm fine now."

"Cause if you want, we could do a quickie before I leave."

Alannah's eyes widened. "Trent."

"I'm serious. You want me to go down on you right now?" He stepped closer.

"No!" She laughed shakily. "It's not necessary."

"You sure? Because I'll do it. I'll do it right now." He dropped his gaze to her hips and licked his lips before lifting his eyes to her face again. She blushed harder. So cute.

"*No*, I'm fine. Thanks for the offer, but I'm good. You handled your business earlier."

"Okay, I just want to make sure you're straight. I'll see you tomorrow, then, okay?"

She nodded and he left after stealing one more kiss.

Alannah closed the door on Trenton and couldn't help the broad smile that spread across her lips. She leaned against the wood, listening for his departure. Two firm knocks made her jump back.

"Hit the deadbolt."

She slid the bolt into place. "Happy now?" she called out, pretending to be annoyed. She rested her forehead against the cool surface of the pine.

He didn't answer right away. Four, maybe five seconds passed.

"Very happy," he said, voice thick and coarse. The same way hers would sound if she dared speak right now. She waited and sensed when he'd moved. Then she heard the truck start and he drove away.

Grinning, Alannah went into the kitchen and put the flowers he brought into a vase she found in a downstairs closet. They looked beautiful sitting on the counter, and in the morning they'd be a nice sight as she ate breakfast.

She couldn't believe Trenton had actually set foot inside a flower shop and picked out flowers. Carnations, no less. Her favorite. She shook her head in disbelief.

Then she went upstairs to change her moist panties.

CHAPTER TWENTY-FIVE

Alannah was fixing a bowl of cereal when the phone rang. Angel popped her head up from the water bowl.

"Who could that be?" she asked the dog, who in turn barked an answer.

She set the milk and cereal on the counter, picked up the phone, and let out a little squeal when she saw the name on the screen. "Hey, Jill!"

Jill was a friend from college and they hadn't spoken in a long time. They'd both been science majors, and while Alannah had remained in Seattle, Jill had accepted a position at the Center for Disease Control and Prevention in Atlanta.

"Hi, Alannah! How are you?" They engaged in a bit of small talk, catching up on the latest with jobs and family before Jill explained the reason for the call. "A couple of months ago, my supervisor mentioned that Emory University Hospital and Georgia Tech are forming a research coalition. At the time, he didn't mention what it was, but I recently found out the coalition is a done deal. They're going to combine the knowledge of the hospital's biomedical research students and engineering students from Georgia Tech. The goal is to—get this—look into making affordable, artificial organs and limbs that are accepted into the human body!"

Jill's voice heightened with excitement the more she talked. "The students do all the work, but they need program managers to supervise them—people with actual practical experience to provide guidance. I immediately thought of you and the work you're doing. Alannah, this is an amazing opportunity. Without an advanced degree, you've probably gone as far as you can go at DymoGenesis. But here, you'd be a supervisor, and the starting pay for a new program manager is in the high six figures. The project has already received funding for five years."

Alannah dropped onto one of the chairs at the bar. "Wow, this does sound like an amazing opportunity." By getting in on the ground floor, she'd have the opportunity to move up as the program grew.

"It *is*. What do you think?"

"I um…I guess I could look into it."

"You don't sound excited. Aren't you interested?"

"I am."

"But…? I thought you'd be happy-*er*."

"I don't have the job yet." Alannah laughed, though her friend was right. She should express more enthusiasm about the potential position. "I don't want to get my hopes up."

"I understand, but I think you'd be perfect for it. You have expertise in the exact same field."

"True." Alannah gnawed on her lip.

She thought about her relationship with Trenton. They'd been seeing each other exclusively over the past two months. Trenton continued to be extremely attentive, making a point of coming up to her job once a week to eat lunch. Depending on how much time he could spare, they ate in the cafeteria or walked to one of the neighboring eateries for sandwiches.

If she applied for and got the job, she'd have to leave Seattle…and him.

"Tell you what," Jill went on, "in a few minutes I'll text the link to where you can look at the details and the requirements for the program manager position. I'll also include the name of my supervisor. If you're interested and apply, use her name as a reference. Okay?"

"Okay."

They chatted for a few minutes more. After they hung up, Alannah sat and stared at the phone until her friend texted the details. When she did, she went right to the link and reviewed the education and work experience requirements.

Jill was right. With her background, she was a perfect fit for the position. It was as if the job description had been written with her in mind.

She rushed upstairs to get her laptop and then sat down at the kitchen counter to fill out the application. Once she'd answered all the questions and uploaded her résumé, she hesitated for a few seconds, the icon hovering over SUBMIT. Then, taking a deep breath, she clicked the button.

"Just to see what happens," she told herself.

The front door opened and Alannah looked up to see Trenton appear in the doorway wearing a pair of distressed jeans and a burnt-orange shirt. He had the sleeves rolled up to right below his elbow, exposing the tats that circled his muscular forearms.

She tapped off the job website and closed the laptop. "What are you doing here? Miss me already?"

Last night she'd had dinner at Canlis fine dining restaurant with him, Ivy and her fiancé, Cyrus and his wife Daniella, and Constance Johnson, their mother. They'd enjoyed a delicious five-course meal in one of the private rooms, with views of Lake Union and the Cascade Mountains in the distance.

He marched over and dropped a kiss on her mouth. "Get dressed. We need to catch a flight in one hour."

"Whoa. Where are we going?"

"New York." He wore an excited grin, which only heightened her curiosity about the out-of-the-blue trip.

"I can't go to New York. I have to work in the morning, and you're supposed to be on your way to Colorado for the beer festival." They'd already said their goodbyes when he left her townhouse this morning. He'd be gone for an entire week.

"I'll have the pilot drop me off in Colorado on the way back from New York, and you'll make it back in time for work in the morning."

Alannah laughed. He'd thought of everything. Holding up her hands, she said, "Slow down. What is this about?"

His features bright and animated, Trenton shook his head. "Can't tell you. It's a surprise."

"Okay, but..." Her eyes dropped to her dog. Angel hadn't barked or even growled once when Trenton showed up. In fact, she hadn't in weeks. Odd. "What about Angel? The kennel's not open on Sunday."

He shrugged. "Can your friend Terri watch her? Or I can get Ivy or Cyrus to take her overnight."

She jabbed a fist onto one hip. "What is this about, Trent?"

"I told you, it's a surprise."

"And I told you, no more gifts."

He'd been spoiling her so much that she'd had to demand he stop giving her gifts—jewelry, clothes, flowers. While flattering, she'd been overwhelmed by the flood of presents. In some ways, she thought he was trying to buy her love and forgiveness, and the truth was, it wasn't necessary.

"This is different. You're going to really, really want it. I promise." He was grinning so hard, some of the excitement started to rub off on her.

"You're spoiling me," she said.

His happy grin turned affectionate and his eyes softened on her. "Is that such a bad thing?"

"No, I guess not."

"Do you trust me?" he asked.

She looked into his eyes. "Yes, I trust you."

"Good. The plane is gassed and waiting for us. Now you need to get ready." He grabbed her by the hand and hauled her from the kitchen.

****

"I can't believe I had dinner with Simon Yam." Alannah squeezed Trenton's hand and released a low-volume squeal.

A lace wrap protected her bare shoulders from the cool

September air. She wore a strapless Donna Karan dress in navy blue and an understated gold and diamond necklace with matching earrings, and had twisted her hair into a loose topknot. Trenton looked delicious in a jacket, white shirt, and no tie.

Their seafood dinner had probably been tasty, but Alannah couldn't remember much about it because she'd been so enthralled by the popular actor. He'd appeared in dozens of films, including one of her favorite thrillers, *The Thieves*. Despite all his complaints about having to read the subtitles of the foreign films, Trenton had been paying attention.

"Simon Sweet Potato is all right," he said.

Alannah punched his arm. "Simon *Yam*. And he's wonderful," she said. The actor had been very gracious and immediately put her at ease with his laid-back, funny conversation.

"I swear you have a crush on this guy. You were giving him googly eyes, and I was sitting right there."

Alannah giggled, blushing. "I was not."

"Yeah, you were." Instead of being angry or jealous, he grinned down at her, clearly pleased with the execution of the surprise.

She leaned into his side, tilting her head to gaze up at him. "How did you arrange this?"

"One of my frat brothers works at the hotel where he's staying, and I'd mentioned in passing how much you liked him and his movies. He was able to get in touch with him and mentioned what a big fan you were." Trenton shrugged.

Alannah gazed up at his profile. "I don't think it was that simple. No doubt you name-dropped who you were and your family, etc."

"I might have mentioned that to his handler." His eyes found hers and he hooked an arm around her neck, pulling her closer and tweaking her freckled nose. She wrinkled it at him and he pressed his lips to her temple, causing her to melt against his muscled frame, relishing the easy affection of the kiss.

A black SUV with tinted windows pulled up, but instead of waiting for the driver to come around, Trenton opened the back door. Alannah slid onto the seat and he followed behind. As they pulled away from the curb, she sidled up beside him and rested her head on his shoulder.

"Can a brother get some room?" he said.

Alannah lifted her head. "Oh, a brother wants some room?" She made a big show of moving away, but Trenton wasn't having it. He dragged her back across the seat and pulled her onto his lap.

"This is dangerous," she said, even though she settled her head on his shoulder. "I should be wearing a seatbelt."

"I'll keep you safe." He closed his arms around her and began to gently rub her back.

"I'm on cloud nine right now," Alannah murmured. She played with a button on his shirt. "You're always doing such nice things for me."

"You deserve it," he said quietly. His hand continued to rub a soothing path up and down her spine.

They remained in the same position, not speaking again until they arrived at the airfield and had to board the private jet. Once they were seated beside each other in the plush leather seats, Alannah reached for his hand.

"Thank you," she said softly.

She saw how much pleasure expressing her appreciation brought him by the way his smile brightened.

"I love you," he said, those three words summing up why he'd gone to all the trouble to arrange this spur-of-the-moment trip.

She ached to say the words back to him, but instead settled for simply resting her head on his shoulder—strong and comfortable, and her favorite spot in the world.

She'd told him she loved him so many times in the past, but now that they were a couple, she was afraid to say the words. Because she wouldn't just be telling him that she loved him. She'd be telling him that she was *in* love with him, and expressing those feelings—at least while sober—scared her.

"Tired?" Trenton asked. She nodded. "Me too. Let's go lie down."

They walked back to the small bedroom, which included a minibar, a TV screen built into a recessed square of the wall, and two chairs on either side of a foldable table that was bolted to the wall.

Trenton sat on the bed and slid his hands under her dress and up her thighs.

"I thought you were tired," she said, as heat circled her core.

"I was, and then you started rubbing all on me."

"I was not." She giggled and pushed him, but he grabbed her around the waist and pulled her close enough to kiss her belly through the dress.

"You wearing the lingerie I bought you?" he whispered.

"Yes."

"You too tired to…?" He raised a brow, and let the question dangle in the middle of the room.

"No."

"Then let me see."

Alannah reached behind her and unzipped the back of the dress. Once undone, it slid into a puddle at her feet. She stood in a bronze strapless bra and panties, both made of satin. He'd chosen them for her, along with a slew of others.

Closing her eyes, she preened under the caress of his hands as they moved slowly up and down the curve of her waist, warming her skin with his gentle touch. Then he kissed her belly button, and in response, her stomach tightened like a coiled spring. She took in a deep breath by mouth and ran her fingers over his head.

His tongue traced a circle around her navel and along the line of the panties. "Love you so much," he whispered. The words seemed torn from him, as he gripped her bottom and squeezed.

Trenton dragged her down on top of him and they enjoyed a hungry, moist kiss. She felt him harden against her thigh and reached down to massage the stiff length of him through his slacks. He moaned, grasping the back of her neck and pushing his tongue past her lips to deepen the kiss.

Alannah unbuttoned his shirt and kissed his throat and chest. Everything about him thrilled and excited her—the golden hue of his skin, the smooth hardness of his body, the way he tasted, even the way he smelled. She could never, ever get enough of Trenton.

She lifted her head and looked down into his handsome face. "I want to be on top."

The green of his eyes darkened and he smiled at her. She smiled back and lowered her head so she could enjoy his luscious mouth again.

****

Before the descent into Colorado, they'd be able to take a few hours' nap.

Lying facing each other, Trenton had his arm thrown across Alannah's waist. She stared at his closed eyes. Even though the festival in Colorado only lasted four days, he'd be gone for an entire week because of the parties and other events taking place around the event. JBC had a big day of grilling and giveaways planned, and the rest of the week he and the reps would be busy, which meant he couldn't talk to her much while there.

Once again, she thought about the job in Atlanta. If offered, could she accept a position across the country, away from Trenton? She didn't think she could. They hadn't even separated for the week yet, and she already missed him.

The truth was, she didn't want a job in Atlanta or anywhere else, for that matter. Not when it meant she'd have to be apart from him.

She touched his face, where tiny bristles had already emerged to roughen his cheek. "I love you," she said quietly.

Although relieved to finally admit her feelings, Alannah experienced the fear and worry of laying bare herself to the one person who could tear her heart in two. A tear slid from the corner of her eye, rolled over her nose, and dripped onto the pillow.

Trenton opened his eyes. Seeing her tear, he lifted a finger and swiped the remnants of it from the bridge of her nose. "Thank you," he said, his voice as quiet as hers.

She smiled and he smiled back. But there was something else underlying the bass in his voice. Something she couldn't quite define at that moment.

Only later, hauled into oblivion by the ropes of sleep, did her subconscious comprehend what she hadn't been able to grasp. It wasn't that he'd said the words thank you, but how he'd said them. The realization tugged at her heart.

He'd sounded so deeply…*grateful.*

Chapter Twenty-six

Alannah sat at Terri's station at the spa, fingers spread out on the table. Terri shook the bottle of nail polish, a color somewhere between pink and lavender. Alannah had already had a facial, all in preparation for Trenton's return.

"I thought the two of you were close before, but now that you're a couple, you're practically inseparable." Terri spread the polish over the first nail. "I can't believe you survived a week without him."

"I can't either," Alannah said. She giggled when Terri shook her head. "I don't think I've ever been happier."

"I don't think I've ever seen you happier." Terri was quiet as she finished the first coat. "So when will you see Mr. Loverman?"

"He flies in this afternoon, but he has to stop at his mother's first. He's going to check on his brother, Gavin."

Terri looked up. "He's the one who had the accident rock climbing in the Andes?"

"That's the one."

Terri shook her head and resumed painting Alannah's nails. "It's like he has a death wish."

Alannah didn't comment. She knew better than to share any information about the Johnsons with anyone, even her good friend. If she could speak about it, she'd tell Terri that Gavin's family didn't approve of his thrill-seeking exploits at all. After her conversation with Trenton, she had a feeling things were about to change for Gavin.

"Okay, all done." Terri closed the bottle.

Alannah spread her fingers and observed her friend's handiwork. "Perfect."

Terri tilted her head. "Your skin is glowing and you're smiling all the time. This relationship agrees with you."

"I think finally getting what I want agrees with me. But sometimes…" She sighed. "I know I'm being ridiculous, but I keep waiting for the other shoe to drop."

Terri frowned. "What do you mean?"

"Some crazy ex-girlfriend, a baby mama, or he'll do something. I dunno." She examined her hands. "It's too perfect. I'm waiting for something to happen to screw it up."

"Nothing's going to happen. That's crazy talk."

Alannah gave her friend a wry smile. "You're right. What am I thinking? We're in a good place. What could possibly happen now?"

****

Trenton walked through his mother's house and into the living room, right on time to hear Cyrus tear into Gavin, who sat in a wheelchair with his right leg stretched out in a cast. There was a brace below his knee on the other leg because of a minor injury he'd sustained to his ankle in his fall in the Andes.

Xavier, the second oldest, who'd recently moved back to Seattle to train under Cyrus, sat on the arm of the sofa with his arms crossed, brows drawn down over his eyes. He looked more polished than Trenton had seen him in years, wearing a charcoal suit and with his long dreadlocks pulled back into a ponytail. He'd begun working directly with Cyrus to take over the day-to-day of the entire Johnson Enterprises conglomerate, and he certainly looked the part of a chief operations officer in training.

"Maybe you get a kick out of risking your life and getting busted up, but none of us want to see that." Cyrus stood over Gavin in a Brioni tuxedo, face tight and voice loud and booming, more reminiscent of their father than Trenton had ever seen him. Cyrus normally remained calm no matter the situation, so seeing him overwrought was unusual. "Mother wants you in Seattle, and you're going to stay here, and that's final."

Cyrus's pregnant wife, Daniella, stood beside him in a dark blue designer evening gown, hair swept up in an elegant style and diamonds around her neck. She placed a calming hand on her husband's shoulder and he stepped back, his mouth tight with frustration.

Ivy stood on the other side of Cyrus. "Gavin, why do you want to leave? You're in no condition to travel. Mother wants you to stay, and while you're here, you have servants and Adelina at your disposal."

"I don't want to be here. Can't you people understand that?" Irritation vibrated in Gavin's voice.

"While you're here, you can recuperate under a good doctor's care—the best money can buy," Ivy pointed out.

"The United States is not the only country with good doctors. I can get excellent medical care in other parts of the world." Gavin's gaze rested on all of them in turn. "I know you guys mean well, but what am I supposed to do for the next couple of months if I stay here?"

"Get a hobby," Cyrus said.

"Without two functional legs?" Gavin looked up at Xavier. "Come on, Xavier. Tell them. They're being ridiculous."

Xavier shook his head. "I'm with Ivy and Cyrus on this one. And anyway, what can you do without two functional legs in another country?"

Gavin sent a silent plea to Trenton with his eyes, but Trenton went to stand with the others. "I agree with them. Besides, it's what Mother wants." Constance Johnson always got her way.

As a last resort, Gavin looked at his sister-in-law. "Daniella, help me out here. Cyrus will listen to you."

Daniella clasped her hands below her protruding belly. "I agree with your family, Gavin. There's absolutely no reason for you to leave. You should stay."

"I don't care what you do to occupy your time," Cyrus said,

clearly still riled up. "Learn to play the piano or the guitar or something. It's up to you, but whatever you do, you'll be doing it from Seattle. At my wife's suggestion, I tried the flies-with-honey approach, and it didn't work. So now I'm telling you, you're not leaving. I'm going to make sure our pilots know you're not allowed to use any of the family aircraft, and Mother's driver will report to me and let me know—"

"As usual, you're being an over-the-top control freak," Gavin fumed.

"And I will make sure that the house manager knows if a hired car or taxi or any unfamiliar vehicle pulls up to the gates, they should not be allowed onto the property."

Gavin glared at his older brother. "Are you serious? You're going to hold me hostage?"

"If that's what it takes. You don't want to take care of yourself, then I will."

"I'm not a child!"

"Then stop acting like one!" Cyrus shouted. They all went silent, and tension, thick and heavy as evening fog, weighed in the air. Cyrus never spoke above a certain decibel. When he continued, his voice had mellowed to a quieter level, but waves of anger still rolled off him. "This isn't a joke, Gavin. Every time you have an accident after one of your ridiculous stunts, we have to sit here and pretend that it's okay. That you'll be fine. You broke your leg in three places. You have bruised ribs and tore up your ankle. It could have been much worse. You could have broken your neck. You could have been killed on that cliff."

Gavin stared down at the floor, his chest heaving in quiet anger. But he didn't respond to Cyrus, because like Trenton, he had to know Cyrus was right. He raced cars, had been skysurfing, BASE jumping, and tackling the waves off Australia's turbulent East Coast. As an adrenalin junkie, his participation in extreme sports had resulted in varying degrees of disasters over the years, yet nothing was off limits.

Cyrus flipped his wrist and looked at the time. He straightened his tie. "Daniella and I have a party to attend." He sounded tired. "If we stay here any longer, we're going to be late. The three of you can deal with him. I'm done." He placed his hand to the small of his wife's back.

"Good night," Daniella said.

They all murmured their goodbyes as the couple left the room.

"What are you going to do?" Ivy asked quietly. "You're being ridiculous. You know that, don't you?"

"*I'm* being ridiculous? Did you hear what our lord and master said?" Gavin shot her a dark look. "I'm an adult. If I want to leave, I should be able to. I should call the police and tell them I'm being held against my will."

"You won't do that," Trenton said.

Gavin sighed heavily and let his head fall backward. He let out a growl. "No, I won't. So I guess I'm stuck here." He rested his head in his hand.

Ivy crossed her arms, her expression holding sadness. "I thought for sure you'd stay a few weeks after my engagement party, but you left after only a few days. Is it so terrible for you to be here?"

Trenton understood why Ivy was so upset. She and Gavin were twins and used to be extremely close—so close they even coordinated their Halloween costumes. He distinctly remembered a party where they'd dressed as the Wonder Twins and another when they'd dressed as Batman and Robin.

"No. It's not so terrible for me to be here," Gavin said in a weary voice.

A glimmer of a smile crossed Ivy's lips. "Stay for a while. Relax."

"Relax. Yeah. I'll try to do that."

"I'll see if I can get some entertainment for you," Trenton offered.

Gavin perked up and smiled slyly. "Would this happen to be female entertainment?"

"Of course."

His eyes lit up. "Does she have a fat ass and big boobs?"

"Of course. I know what you like."

Both men chuckled knowingly.

"Oh goodness." Ivy rolled her eyes. "That's my cue to leave."

She leaned down to give her brother a hug. When she stood up, she was smiling. "This isn't exactly the condition I wanted you in, but I'm glad you're back for a while, so I'll take you any way I can get you. Bye, Trent. Bye, Xavier." She waved on her way out.

"I'm out, too," Xavier said.

"Where are you going?" Gavin asked.

"Mind your business." Xavier walked out with a smirk on his face.

Gavin waited until he and Trenton were alone. With a twinkle in his eyes, he said, "Speaking of fat asses…how's Alannah?"

"Don't start."

Gavin chuckled. "I won't, I won't. I know that's your girl now. About time, too. I can't believe how long the two of you were doing the friend thing."

"Yeah…well, sometimes you can't see what's right under your nose."

"True. So is it serious? You're off the market?"

Trenton nodded.

"Damn."

Trenton laughed at his brother's raised eyebrows.

"Who'll be my partner in crime now?"

"You'll have to find somebody else. I'm not screwing this up."

"Good for you. She's a good woman."

"Speaking of which, I better get out of here. I haven't seen her in a week, and she's meeting me at my place later." He clapped Gavin on the shoulder and his brother winced in pain. "Sorry about that. Stay out of trouble."

"Yeah, yeah."

Chapter Twenty-seven

She should have written a list.

Alannah reviewed the items in her hand basket at Aldi's Market, a Seattle-based specialty grocer. The owner, a French Arab from Morocco, imported a huge selection of gourmet foods. On any given night, there may be tastings for the latest imported Argentinean wines accompanied by a selection of artisanal cheeses. Tonight she'd sampled the caviar and foie gras, but her basket contained the fixings for dinner—organic chicken, fresh herbs, heavy cream, cheese, and pasta.

Angel was at the kennel, so Alannah could stay the night and all day tomorrow with Trenton. He had dinner covered tonight with an order from The Best Thai Restaurant. They could go out to dinner tomorrow, but she wanted to spend a lazy Sunday afternoon with him, and had an idea for a chicken dish she was certain he'd enjoy.

"I guess that's all I need," she murmured to herself.

On the way to the cashiers, she saw a man in the aisle. Stocky, average height, and with a circle beard. As she neared he looked up, eyes narrowing when they rested on her. She kept moving and had passed him when he spoke.

"Hey. You're Trenton Johnson's girlfriend, right?"

Alannah paused and turned to look at the stranger. Since she didn't know this person or his motives, she was immediately cautious. "Something like that."

He laughed. "Don't be coy. Trenton makes it very obvious that you are not to be messed with. Stay away. Hands off." He held up both hands, palms facing outward.

"Really?" He was staking claims like that?

"Yeah. I'm Steve, by the way." He extended his hand.

They shook hands. "Alannah."

"I know who you are. Everybody knows who you are." He looked her up and down in a decidedly non-friendly way.

Alannah slid her hand from his. "Well, it was nice to—"

"Trenton didn't want me asking about you—didn't even want me looking at you. He almost chewed my head off over you."

"Oh. He can be a little…protective."

"That was three months ago. He's probably even worse now."

Alannah frowned. "Three months ago? You must have the time wrong." That would have been June, and she and Trenton had only become a couple in July.

"No, ma'am, I'm not mistaken. You probably didn't see me, but it was one night when he played at The Underground. I never saw the performance because he had me kicked out."

"Are you sure?" They weren't together then, but the last time Trenton had played at the club had been in June.

"Oh I'm sure, sweetheart. You had on a red minidress. You looked nice. Real nice."

Alannah had the distinct impression this guy didn't understand the concept of boundaries. Still, what he said didn't make sense. "And Trenton told you he and I were together? Back in June?"

"Oh yeah. After I paid you a compliment, he said I should keep my eyes to myself—or something along those lines. I couldn't believe the brother went off like that just for looking. But my friend, Julian, explained later that he's always been that way about you."

Alannah couldn't believe what she was hearing. "Always?"

"You didn't know? Your man does not play, sweetheart. Brothers know to stay the hell away from you. If you want to stay out of trouble, you stay the hell away from Trenton Johnson's woman."

Steve rubbed his chin and looked her up and down again. "Makes me wonder why he feels he has to stand guard like that."

The lustful look in his eyes made her skin crawl. "I better go."

"Nice talking to you. Tell your man I said hi."

Alannah rushed down the aisle toward the front of the store, knowing the entire time Steve watched her walk away.

And knowing that she had to confront Trenton.

****

Alannah sat in Trenton's living room, waiting. Five minutes ago he had texted that he was five minutes away. She'd already unpacked the groceries and spent time reviewing the conversation with Steve in her head. Nothing he had said made any sense.

The door opened and she rose to greet Trenton.

He came in wearing dark slacks and a white button-down shirt, and dropped his suitcase and carry-on against the wall. "Honey, I'm home."

He danced over, his sexy hips moving from side to side and that adorable, lopsided smile lifting the right corner of his mouth. He held up a plastic sack in his hand. "Look at what I got," he said, waving it in front of her. "He threw in extra basil rolls. That dude loves you. He's lucky I'm not a jealous man and I know you're all mine." He leaned down and pulled her into a kiss.

A week apart had left Alannah thirsting for his touch. She lifted her lips and almost succumbed to the warmth of his embrace and the flavor of his mouth, but she held back.

Trenton lifted his head. "What's wrong?"

She licked her lips, a little afraid of the outcome of the conversation. "You said you're not a jealous man."

"Well, I am a little bit, but I know he doesn't mean any harm." He grinned and went into the kitchen. "Guess who won the gold medallion in the specialty beer category at the festival?"

"Johnson Brewing Company?" She stared down at her hands, summoning the courage to confront him.

"That's right. Hey, you want to eat first or have smoking-hot-I-missed-Trenton sex first? I'm leaving the decision up to you, but I strongly recommend option number two."

Alannah went to stand in the entryway of the kitchen. "So if he meant harm, you would…what?"

Trenton pulled a bottle of water from the refrigerator. "What are we talking about?"

"Aat, at The Best Thai Restaurant. You said you know he doesn't mean any harm, but what if he did? What would you do?"

"Nothing. I feel like you're leading up to something. Like I'm being baited." He tipped the bottle back and took a big gulp.

"You're right. Why play around, when I should come right out and ask you." They looked at each other from across the room, and Alannah pushed past the knots in her stomach. "Have the regulars at The Underground always thought I was your girlfriend?"

He stared blankly at her, and she could almost see him thinking, wondering what to admit or deny. "Why are you asking me that?" Her question required a simple yes or no, and the fact that he didn't reply with either actually provided an answer. He didn't even act shocked or surprised or deny.

"I saw this guy at Aldi's. His name is Steve."

"Steve who?"

"I don't know his last name. He said he'd been to The Underground and mentioned Julian. I guess he's a friend of yours—"

"He's not my friend." His face cemented into an emotionless mask.

"I guess not, since you had him kicked out of the club." Alannah kept her eyes on him, watching every movement of his eyes and body. "Did you tell men at the club to stay away from me?"

He set the bottle of water on the counter and scrubbed a hand across his jaw. "Not really. Not in so many words."

"So why did he get that impression, Trent? He said it's *always* been that way."

Trenton cursed softly and took a deep breath. "I never actually told anyone to stay away from you—well, except him. I guess…I let everybody else think whatever they wanted."

Her heart beat faster. "Which was…?"

"Lana—"

"Which was?"

He rubbed the back of his neck. "That you were off limits. That there was something going on between us."

Her lips parted in shock. "Wow. And they thought that because we were always together."

"I guess." He shrugged.

"You guess? So let me get this straight, all along these people think I'm your girlfriend, but you go to the club and pick up women right under my nose? You made me look like a brainless twit. The kind of woman who'll put up with anything. Heck, the kind of women I've warned you to avoid but you can't seem to get enough of."

"It's not as bad as you think," Trenton said quietly.

"Yes it is! All this time, no one talked to me because they thought I was with you. Even that night, when I had my hair done and a brand new outfit, you knew and you didn't say anything? You were scaring men away from me?"

"That night…the way you were dressed…" He shook his head. "Guys like Steve only want one thing."

"You had no right to do that. Why did you do that to me?"

"You know why."

"No, I honestly don't."

"I love you," he said simply. "I loved you then."

"That's not love!" Alannah shrieked. "Love doesn't deceive and lie."

Trenton swallowed and spoke in a soothing voice. "I understand you're upset."

"You have no idea." Alannah took a tremulous breath. "I've spent my whole life—our entire friendship—worried about your needs, and you've spent our entire friendship worried about your needs. I've been all about you and you've been all about you."

Color tinged his cheeks. "That's not true. You know that's not true."

He was right, but she was angry and hurt and disillusioned by his actions. She couldn't stop talking if someone suddenly stuck duct tape over her mouth.

"You knew how hurt I was that night. You saw how upset I was that no one even tried to talk to me, yet you pretended to be my friend, pretended to care, and the entire time it was your fault." Anger and disappointment burned a path through her veins. "My friend Jill told me about a great job in Atlanta."

He became very still. "Why are you telling me about a job in Atlanta?"

"Because I applied for it. It's a great opportunity."

He pushed away from the counter, nostrils flaring. "You have a good job here. Why do you want to work way down there? Atlanta is on the other side of the goddamn country."

"Because I'm tired of my life revolving around you. You can't even be honest with me."

"And you were honest with me?" he shot back. "Sneaking around behind my back and applying for a job all the way in Atlanta? What's the matter, you couldn't find one in Timbuktu?"

"Nice, Trent. Now you're trying to make me into the bad guy, but I had every right to apply for that job. Let's get back to what this conversation is about. The truth. And the truth is, *you're* part of the reason I've been unhappy for so long." Alannah pressed a hand to her forehead. "I'm so stupid."

"You're being ridiculous and blowing this out of proportion."

She looked up at him. "I trusted you. You're my best friend. But all these years you've been pissing a circle around me, claiming you want to protect me. That's all well and good, but who's been protecting me from you?"

Trenton didn't answer right away, his mouth drawing into a tight line and his body stiffly rejecting her words. "You don't need protecting from me," he finally said in a grim tone.

"Yes, I do. I need protecting from you, and I need to get away from you, your family, everything. Everything I've known, because you know what? I don't know anything else. My life is too wrapped up in yours. I've been living my life for you. How sad is that?" *Me and Trent.* Every story about any major event in her life began with those three words. "I need to make my own memories, without you being involved."

Alannah marched back into the living room and headed for the front door.

"Where are you going?"

She turned to see Trenton staring at her, no longer happy, no longer smiling. Tension radiated from his body.

"Away from you."

CHAPTER TWENTY-EIGHT

Their relationship was still in a cool stage. In the past two weeks, they'd seen each other twice—once for lunch and another time when they'd attended a party together.

Guarded and stilted, they barely touched. Alannah wasn't sure what she wanted to do. She didn't want to break up with him, but at the same time, she didn't think their relationship was a healthy one.

When she received an invitation to go to Atlanta for the job interview, she sent a group text to Trenton, her family, and Terri. Her sisters and Terri texted back their congratulations right away, and her parents called to wish her well.

She didn't hear from Trenton until that night.

Congratulations. When is the interview?

Monday.

A full hour passed before he replied. *Knock em dead.*

He wasn't trying to stop her, so she should be happy. Yet she wasn't.

The doorbell rang. Alannah set the book she'd been reading on the coffee table and rolled off the couch. She peeked out the window, a little disappointed when she saw Terri. Of course it wouldn't be Trenton. He'd promised to give her space so she could "make her own memories," and he was certainly sticking to his promise.

Alannah opened the door.

"Hey, honey. I hope you don't mind me stopping by unannounced."

"No, come on in."

They went into the living room and Alannah pulled the fleece throw over her legs.

"What're you reading?" Terri asked, brushing hair from her face. Tonight her hair was parted in the middle.

Alannah showed her the cover. "A book that offers tips on how to ace an interview. They include sample questions and suggestions on how to answer them."

"Oh." Terri folded her legs beneath her on the couch. "Listen, we need to talk about you and Trenton. You know I never understood your relationship with him. I've told you before I thought the two of you are weirdly codependent even though you were supposedly just friends."

"Yes, I know. Where are you going with this?"

"I only said that because I want to make it clear that what I'm about to say is completely without bias."

Alannah waited.

"Trenton's behavior sounds like a classic case of man logic."

"And what is man logic?" Terri considered herself an expert on men, so her answer should be interesting.

"Basically, a man does something so ridiculous, it doesn't make sense to the average woman, but makes perfect sense to the man in question." She waited for the explanation to sink in before she continued. "He didn't mean to hurt you."

"That doesn't make what he did okay."

"I know that and you know that. But in his own crazy way, he was keeping other men away from you, even though he wouldn't be with you and was nailing every piece of tail that shook her ass at him. But in man logic, that makes perfect sense, because he was keeping you for himself, and he didn't mean to hurt you."

"That's cute, but if that's the case, man logic sucks."

"I know. It's the reason the world is so messed up today." A soft, sympathetic smile graced her features.

"I'm still going to Atlanta. I have to see what other opportunities there are for me." Alannah picked at her fingernails. "I've made decisions around Trent all my life. It's sad, it's pathetic, and I don't want to do that anymore. Who knows what I've been missing out on because I've been so caught up in him? What if there's another man out there for me? Someone who I'm more in tune with?"

"But you've had boyfriends over the years."

"Yes, but have I really given them a chance when I've basically been in love with Trent my entire life? When he calls, I answer. When he needs me, I'm there. There's got to be something different. Someone different. In a new environment I can explore my options in a way I haven't before, because I won't be distracted by my feelings for Trent."

Terri's eyes filled with sympathy and understanding. "If getting a job on the opposite side of the country is what you need to do to feel better, then do it. But honey, I don't think that's going to make a difference."

"I've got to do something. Even if I don't feel better, I…at least I'll be living. Right?"

"Yeah." But Terri's lackluster response didn't sound genuine. It sounded like she was saying what was necessary to make Alannah believe she'd made a sound decision. "If you get that job, I'm going to miss you, though. What about me?" She poked out her bottom lip.

"I'll miss you, too, but it'll be nice to see what it's like somewhere else." Alannah dog-eared a page in the book and closed it. "I've lived in Seattle all my life. It might be nice to start over, y'know?"

"I know. I had to do it myself once. That's why I left Atlanta." She clutched Alannah's hand. "Is it wrong that I hope you don't get the job?"

"Yes, Terri."

Her friend smiled. "In that case, good luck."

****

October sixteenth.

Alannah paused on the way out the door to answer her cell phone.

"Alannah, hi. Is Trent with you?" Ivy's worried voice came through the line.

Alannah felt terrible. She'd hesitated for far too long on whether or not she should go to Trenton. She thought maybe he wouldn't want to see her, but hearing the anxiety in his sister's voice confirmed she was doing the right thing.

"No, but I'm on my way to his place now."

"Oh good." Relief flooded Ivy's voice.

In the background, she heard a male voice ask, "What did she say?"

Ivy covered the mouthpiece, and a muted conversation ensued before Cyrus's commanding voice came on the line. "As soon as you confirm he's at home, call Ivy or text her so we know he's all right. He hasn't answered his phone all evening. Ivy and I are out of town, and so is Xavier. Mother's been trying to reach Trenton but can't. She's ready to go over there to check on him if need be."

Trenton usually worked through the anniversary of his parents' death in his own way, which often meant that she spent as much time as she could with him. If the sixteenth fell on a workday, he took the day off, but whatever he did, his family never worried because they knew she and Trenton were together.

They must know they were barely on speaking terms, and Trenton must really be suffering if he hadn't even returned the calls from his mother.

Alannah exited her apartment. "Tell Miss Constance I'm on my way over there right now, and I'll send a text when I see him."

"Thank you, Alannah."

"No problem. I'll be in touch very soon."

In the Lexus, she pressed the gas pedal to the floor and allowed the car to accelerate as much as she could without the risk of being pulled over for reckless driving. The fact that Trenton was unreachable worried her immensely. Just as she wasn't sure he wanted to hear from her, he obviously didn't feel comfortable calling her, even though she knew he hated spending the day alone.

At the building, she rode the elevator up to his floor and entered the penthouse. When the doors slid open, the lights didn't automatically come on in the vestibule like they normally did. The interior of the condo was quiet and dark, but the distant hum of the television called her back to Trenton's bedroom. She walked down the hallway and past the open door to the music room where he practiced the violin in front of the sweeping views of the floor-to-ceiling windows. She found him propped against a bunch of pillows stacked along the metal bars of the bed, watching the movie *Shaft*.

He knew the dialogue by heart, and so did she. It was a favorite of his father's and they watched it every year.

He didn't look up. "What are you doing here?"

"It's October sixteenth."

"So?" The television screen flashed light intermittently across his drawn face.

"I'm not arguing with you."

Alannah pulled out her phone and sent a text to his sister, letting her know she was at Trenton's and he was fine. A *Thank you!!!* was immediately returned.

"What are you doing?" He looked at the phone in her hand.

"Your family was worried and they called me. I sent a text to let them know you're all right. Don't you have your phone on?"

He returned his gaze to the television. "No."

Alannah slipped off her shoes and tossed her coat and purse on one of the chairs in the room. She climbed into the bed and pulled the covers up to her waist.

"How's your head?" She gently ran a hand across his forehead, over the top of his head and down to his nape.

"Okay."

"Did you have to take anything?" He never failed to get a stress headache if he thought too much about that day.

"Ibuprofen."

After a while, he asked, "You staying the night?" He tried to sound nonchalant, pretending not to need her, but she knew him well enough to know that wasn't true.

Despite the cool awkwardness between them, she couldn't let him be alone tonight of all nights. He'd managed to conceal his grief in recent years, but she'd never forget the year he'd been depressed and gotten stinking, sloppy drunk. The pain of his loss and the torment of the memories had been written on his face as clearly as the ink that marked his flesh. He'd been so wounded. So broken. She never wanted to see him like that again.

She placed her head on his shoulder, and after a moment's hesitation, he laid his head on hers.

"Yes. I'm staying the night."

He visibly relaxed as tension eased from his body.

****

The next morning, Alannah and Trenton stood in his kitchen drinking coffee. He rested a hip against the counter with a white mug in his hand, watching her.

She hadn't slept so comfortably in a long time. Her thoughts never gave her any rest at night, but spending the night spooning with Trenton had put her mind at ease.

He wore a pair of black bedroom slippers and black pajama bottoms and left his chest bare, such an unjust act. He looked deliciously scruffy with a new growth of hair on his face and his hard chest and tatted arms exposed to her hungry eyes. She wanted to go over there and lean on him and rub his rough jaw. He would smell like Trenton and morning sleep and comfort. Holding tight to the mug in her own hand helped her resist the urge.

"You're still leaving for Atlanta, aren't you?" he asked.

She nodded. "It's a good opportunity."

"So you said."

"Because it is."

He looked down into the mug of coffee and then looked back up at her with bleak eyes. "Why are you punishing me like this?" he asked in a strained voice.

Alannah's heart hurt at the expression on his face. "I'm not punishing you."

"Like hell you're not."

"My decision has nothing to do with you. I want to find out more about the job. This is about me, for a change."

He stared down into his mug again, and the silence stretched between them to an almost untenable degree before he spoke. "I could pull some strings and get you a better job here." His eyes found hers, sorrowful and pain-filled. "Why don't I do that? I could talk to some people, or someone in my family is bound to know someone. We could try that research center the Johnson Foundation donates millions to every year. What's its name?" He double-snapped his fingers. "You know the one I'm talking about. I could get you a job in their lab. Or—or we could try a biotech company. Let me make some calls—"

"*Trenton.*"

Quiet descended on the room.

He looked steadily at her. "Tell me the job you want, Alannah. I'll get it for you."

She took a deep breath. "You're not listening."

"I am listening."

"No, you're not. I don't want you to buy me a job or use your name to get me one. I won't allow it."

He set his mug down and gripped the edge of the counter. Muscles protruded from under his skin like thick ropes of cable wire. "What good is my name and money if I can't use them to hold on to the most important thing in my life?"

A dart of pain grazed her heart. She placed her cup on the stove. She hadn't even tasted the coffee. The cup had been a prop to get her through the morning's awkwardness.

She had to leave because his words were weakening her resolve. "I'm gonna head out," she said, but didn't move.

Neither of them moved. Neither of them spoke. Misery hung over the room like an ominous cloud before a thunderstorm.

"What time do you leave on Monday?"

"I don't leave on Monday, I leave tomorrow."

His head whipped in her direction, his green eyes filled with surprise. "You said your interview is on Monday."

"It is, but I booked my flight for Sunday. It's an afternoon flight, nonstop to Atlanta."

"Were you going to tell me?"

"Yes, of course." Alannah twisted her hands together. "I'm going to crash at Jill's place and go to the interview on Monday. I'll be back on Wednesday. We haven't seen each other in years, so we're going to hang out a little bit."

"So that's it, then? I can't change your mind?"

"It's a great opportunity," she said again. This was the right decision for her, and she couldn't allow his feelings to factor into her decision-making.

"Lana, I'm sorry," he said, making a last-ditch effort to change her mind. "I'm really, really sorry."

"I know."

"No, you don't know. You don't know how sorry I am. You don't know how much I regret what I did. I promise I'll make it up to you. Just give me a chance." His hands turned into fists, the tendons in his neck tightening. "You know I can't…I can't bear to be without you, but that's what you're threatening me with. You want to punish me, fine. I'll do the time, but it can't be that. You can't leave me."

Alannah briefly closed her eyes. "Stop, please," she begged. She started to move away, but with a few long strides he was across the floor and grabbed her arm.

"You love me, don't you?"

"You know I do," she said softly.

He clasped her hands in both of his, naked pain and frustration marring his face. "Okay, then. I love you, too. That's why I did those stupid things. It wasn't out of maliciousness and it wasn't to hurt you. I know that's what I did, but it wasn't my intent. I lied because I love you. I've loved you almost all my life, and I was just—I didn't know how to deal with those feelings, that's all. But—but I know now. Give me another chance. You won't regret it."

Shaking her head against the temptation to give in, she said, "That's no excuse for what you did. You know that, Trent. Put yourself in my shoes. How would you feel if you knew I'd been secretly sabotaging you?"

"I'd forgive you," he said without hesitation.

"I've forgiven you, too. But that doesn't change the fact that I need to look into the program manager position. This has nothing to do with you. It's about me."

"Then you haven't really forgiven me."

"I have, but my decision can't be based on what you want. This is about me. I don't know how many more ways to tell you the same thing."

His hands fell away to his sides, leaving her devoid of his warm touch. "So I guess that's it."

"I guess so," she said.

"I'll be seeing you." He turned away from her, walked back to the counter, and picked up his coffee. He took a sip, and when he set it down, his profile was hard and tight.

"Bye," Alannah whispered, suddenly unsure of her decision. Maybe leaving was the wrong choice to make, but if she didn't go, she'd never know for sure.

Trenton didn't respond, his head bent and eyes trained on the counter. With nothing left to say, she quietly left his kitchen, left his penthouse, and headed home.

CHAPTER TWENTY-NINE

Seated in the leather chair in his office, Trenton stared out at the city. Practicing the violin for an hour last night hadn't offered any reprieve from his thoughts, so he'd come in to work that morning to take his mind off Alannah's departure.

Behind him, Dave, the eager as ever and verbose sales rep who happened to be working today, too—the guy really needed to get a life—droned on and on about what he hoped to accomplish next year. He'd written up a detailed report of his experience at Munich's Oktoberfest and had a bullet list two pages long of ideas and suggestions for improvement. Trenton hardly caught a word he said, and the fact that he wasn't even looking at him didn't slow Dave down.

Trenton rubbed a hand across his jaw. He'd been hurt before, of course. Who hadn't? Back in college, a crush on a studious girl had ended when she told him in blunt terms that he was *not* her type. But the pain he'd experienced back then couldn't compare to the bone-crushing loss he felt now. Over the years, no matter whom he'd dated or slept with, Alannah remained the constant woman in his life. His rock.

And he couldn't breathe without her. That simple. As if someone had hefted ballast on his chest and then sat on it for good measure.

Trenton rubbed his sternum to ease the pressure, and the corners of his mouth lifted into a self-deprecating smirk. He'd always thought sappy crap like that was ridiculous when he heard people say it. Yet he'd be damned if he didn't feel like he was suffocating.

He swiveled around in the chair and stood. "I have to go."

Dave halted the rapid flow of words. "Oh. Should I leave you a copy of my ideas?"

"Sure, and we can discuss them in more detail sometime this week. Get with my assistant tomorrow and have her slot you in for thirty minutes on my calendar. However, I have to get out of here right now. It's a bit of an emergency."

Dave stood. "That sounds great. I, um—"

"Thanks, Dave." Trenton came around the desk and clapped him on the shoulder. "You're doing an incredible job, and bringing you on board was one of the best decision we've ever made."

Dave beamed. "Thank you, sir."

"No problem. Now I hate to kick you out, but I have got to get out of here." He said it all with a smile.

"Gotcha."

Dave walked ahead of him, and Trenton clutched his keys. He'd do whatever it took to change Alannah's mind. He didn't have much of a plan except to beg her not to…actually, he just planned to beg.

****

On the ride to the airport, Trenton tried to reach Alannah. She had her phone turned off, but he stayed positive. He didn't know on which airline she'd booked a flight, but he narrowed down the choices once he figured out which ones had nonstop legs to Atlanta and which one she was most likely to take.

He pulled into short-term parking at the airport and then hurried to the terminal. Quickly scanning the passengers, he didn't see her or the easy-to-recognize design of the Louis Vuitton luggage he'd gifted her a couple of years ago. Risking the anger of people in line, he walked up to the counter of the first airline he thought she might have taken, and interrupted one of the ticket agents.

He flashed the same easygoing smile that usually got him his way. "Excuse me, I need to find out if there's a passenger scheduled to fly with you and whether or not she's checked in yet."

The woman looked up at him but immediately looked back down at the computer screen. "I'm sorry, sir, but we can't divulge that information."

Trenton was pretty sure if she wasn't so busy, that first try would have gone better. He laughed, resting an elbow on the counter and affecting a friendly, relaxed pose—trying to come across as less panicked than he felt. "I realize there must be some kind of confidentiality laws or something that have to be adhered to, but this is an emergency. I just need to know if she's checked in or not. That's all."

The agent handed the passenger at the counter a boarding pass and the man walked away. "Mr.…?"

"Johnson," he answered quickly. "Trenton Johnson."

Blank stare. Did she not know who he was?

"Mr. Johnson, we have a line."

He'd literally met the one woman in Seattle he couldn't charm. Today of all days.

Trenton stood up straight and his jaw firmed. "Do you know who I am? Do you know who my family is?" He'd never before pulled the Johnson card and sounded like a self-important ass, but he didn't give a shit. He needed information. Now.

They locked eyes.

"Should I?" she asked.

Trenton clenched his teeth. "I want to speak to your supervisor. *Now.*"

"Whoever you think you are—"

"I'll help you, Mr. Johnson." The young woman at the next terminal smiled nervously, blue eyes darting between him and her coworker. Trenton's gaze dropped to her name tag. Her name was Lola.

"What are you doing?" the other agent hissed.

"He's a member of the Johnson family," Lola said from the corner of her mouth, as if Trenton couldn't hear her. "They own restaurants and Johnson Brewing Company. They employ thousands of people and donate millions to charity every year. I think we can make an exception." She flashed a wide smile at Trenton. "Which passenger did you need me to check on?"

Trenton slanted a glance at the other agent's red face before giving Lola his undivided attention. "Alannah Bailey." He spelled her first and last name. "She was scheduled to go out on a flight to Atlanta, but I don't know which one."

"Not a problem. One moment please." Her fingers ran across the keyboard in a series of rapid clicks. "I see she was scheduled to leave on the two-thirty flight to Atlanta, and she did check in."

Trenton glanced at the clock behind the ticket counter. Two forty.

Damn. Alannah was already on her way to the job interview that was a "great opportunity."

He should have left the office earlier. If he had, he might have caught her and been able to talk her out of going. No doubt she'd get the job once she impressed the interviewers with her intelligence and knowledge.

The crushing, suffocating feeling returned full force.

Trenton ran a hand over his head. "Thank you," he mumbled.

He shoved his hands into his coat pockets and trudged toward the exit. Outside, the cool air hit him in the face, and he stopped for a moment, trying to catch his breath. He looked left, right, and that was when he saw her. Seated on a metal bench in a heather-gray peacoat, hands folded in her lap, and a Louis Vuitton rolling carry-on beside her.

The invisible band that had tightened around his chest loosened a fraction, and Trenton gratefully dragged fresh, cool air into his lungs. He walked over to the bench and sat next to Alannah.

Neither of them said anything. They watched passengers disembark from vehicles, and new arrivals pile luggage into the trunks of cars.

Alannah looked at him with red-rimmed eyes. "What are you doing here?"

"You should have the experience you want, away from me. I know that, but I still couldn't let you go without making one more effort to change your mind." He took her smaller hand in both of his. "Why didn't you leave?"

She shifted her gaze to the passengers being dropped off and picked up. "I checked in and then thought, why waste their time? Why waste my time, when I already know that if they offer me the job, I won't accept it. Because it'll take me away from you." Slowly, she shook her head. "I couldn't do it. I couldn't leave. No matter where I go, to the other side of the country or even to the other side of the world, my heart belongs to you. I don't want to be anyplace you aren't. Right here, with you, is where I want to be."

He squeezed her cool fingers between his. "I really do regret what I did."

"I know."

He ran a fingertip over her middle finger, from the nail to the knuckle. "I used to think the worst thing that ever happened to me was seeing my mother kill my father and then turn the gun on herself. But I recovered from that. It took a long time, but I did. I even got a new family, new friends, and a new life to help me cope. But if I lose you…" His voice thickened. "If I lose you, if I don't have you in my life, I don't think I can recover. There's no coping, no getting by, no 'I'll be okay.' Because no one can ever take your place, Lana. Women are everywhere, but you—you're different. You're special. You're my best friend, and I need you in my life."

"Why do you have to say stuff like that?" She dropped her head on his shoulder, and he inhaled the familiar scent of her hair and skin.

He smiled. "I say stuff like that because it's true." Trenton bent his head to hers and they bumped noses. Her eyes smiled into his. "It's true," he repeated, his voice thick with emotion. "You're irreplaceable. I love you. You believe me, don't you?"

"I do." She sighed. "You and your crazy man logic."

"My what?"

"Nothing." She smiled with her lips, her eyes, her entire face. "Just kiss me."

Happy to oblige, Trenton pressed his mouth against her soft, cool lips. When she leaned into him, he cupped her jaw in his hand

and deepened the connection, barely holding back from ravishing her right there on the sidewalk.

When their lips separated, he stroked her jaw with his thumb. Looking deeply into her eyes, he asked, "No regrets?"

"No regrets. I realize that I made my decision a long, long time ago. I chose you, Trent. I'll always choose you."

Trenton kissed the palm of her hand. He could smell the candy-apple sanitizer, arguably the most alluring scent in the world, solely because it represented Alannah.

Standing, he picked up her suitcase. "Ready?" He extended his hand.

"Yes." She closed her fingers around his and rose to her feet.

And followed behind him, the way she'd always done. Ever since they were eight years old.

Chapter Thirty

Trenton trailed Alannah up the stairs and set her suitcase in the closet. Then he turned his attention to the woman he loved. She stood in the middle of the room, silently watching him. He walked over and proceeded to slowly undress her, taking the time to release each button on her coat.

He tossed it aside and then lowered to his haunches to remove her shoes. Once she'd stepped out of them, he slipped the long-sleeved blouse over her head. Pants, socks, and underwear followed.

Then it was her turn to undress him.

"I guess we'll always be stuck with each other," he said.

"Is that how you feel? Stuck?" She unzipped his pants.

"Nah." He tilted her head up so he could see her eyes. "Does it ever scare you? To need someone so much."

She paused with her fingers on the middle button of his shirt. "Yes. Does it scare you?"

"A little. But we can be scared together." He grinned.

She grinned back. "Considering everything we've been through over the years, I think we can handle this."

"Agreed."

They fell onto the bed and their naked bodies wrapped around each other. Comfortable. Familiar.

"We haven't made love since before I left for Colorado," Trenton reminded her. He said the words against her arched throat, his fingers strumming her clit as deftly as he did the strings of the violin. "That's cruel and unusual punishment. It's unconstitutional."

Her laughter was breathless and husky, and utterly content. A sound that he wanted to hear many more times to come.

He made love to her in an unrushed, leisurely fashion. Taking his time, he let his fingers sweep over her soft hair and skin, leaving not an inch of flesh untouched. His tongued traced the line of vertebrae from the small of her back to the base of her neck. And his mouth savored the moisture of desire between her legs, until she cried out, trembling, and clamped her thighs around his head.

When their bodies joined together, she allowed him deeper than she ever had, crossing her ankles high up on his back. Her forearms tightened around his neck and held him close, and his eardrums filled with the sound of her whimpers and breathless pants.

She climaxed and he groaned, burying his face in her neck, the tremors that shook her body echoing within him as he released.

He whispered the first words that came to mind—the only words he could say after such an intense orgasm and the relief of holding on to the love of his life. "Love you so much, Alannah."

Then he took a deep breath, and the remaining tightness in his chest completely dissipated.

****

The ringing phone broke through Alannah's sleep, and she felt the loss of heat as Trenton rolled away from her. He slapped his hand along the table in the dark and finally found the phone.

"Hello?" He was quiet for a bit and then he sounded alarmed when he said, "What? And you're just now calling me?"

Alannah rolled to face him. "What is it?" she asked, still groggy from sleep.

"Daniella went into early labor eight hours ago," Trenton whispered. He put the phone on speaker.

"At first they thought it was another false alarm," Ivy explained. "Then they wanted to wait until she was properly dilated before calling anyone. She's in the delivery room now. Our nephew will be here any minute."

Trenton swung his legs over the side of the bed. "We're on our way."

"You don't have to rush. Come when you're ready."

"We'll be there soon."

He and Alannah dressed, while she chattered excitedly about the baby. No surprise, since she loved babies and spoiled her niece and nephews rotten. Now she'd have another baby to love on.

By the time they arrived at the hospital, Michael Andrew had already made his appearance. Flowers and balloons filled the large room where the family was located, in a private wing reserved for celebrity and high-profile births.

Phone pressed to her ear, Ivy waved hello as she updated her fiancé, Lucas, who'd stayed at home with their daughter. Daniella, looking drained, greeted them with a wan smile and wave from the bed. Cyrus sat in a chair, holding her hand and talking quietly to her. With Xavier still out of town, the only other immediate family member missing was Gavin. Alannah figured because of his limited mobility he'd decided to stay at home.

She went over to the bassinet where the family matriarch, Constance Johnson, stood over her new grandson. As always, the older woman wore a tailored designer dress and her shoulder-length hair was perfectly styled without a strand out of place.

"He's adorable," Alannah whispered, so as not to wake the baby.

"Yes, he is. How are you?" Constance asked. She searched Alannah's face and shot a quick glance across the room at Trenton. "I see everything is back to normal."

"Yes, ma'am." Alannah's cheeks heated with color.

"Good." She patted Alannah's hand.

Less than an hour after their brief exchange, four more people arrived—two men and two women. She knew Hudson Lynch, the Johnson family's spokesperson. His PR firm handled all their media relations. He had striking blue eyes and sported a fake tan, with his long hair pulled back into a ponytail. She soon learned that the other man was a photographer and the two women a hair stylist and makeup artist.

Alannah watched in amazement as the stylist whipped Daniella's hair into a tamed style that fell over one shoulder, looking sleek and neat but not overdone. The makeup artist worked the same magic on her face, using concealer and neutral colors to give her a fresh-faced look that didn't appear made up.

When they'd completed their work, Constance carefully lifted the baby from the bassinet and handed him to Daniella. The photographer proceeded to take a slew of photos. Close-ups of the baby, pictures of Daniella and the baby, photos of Cyrus, Daniella, and the baby, and even photos of the entire group gathered together.

Having been close with the family for so long, Alannah knew the purpose of everything they did was not only to capture the moment for the family. They would release official photos to the press so as to avoid the feeding frenzy that could ensue when media outlets jockeyed to get the first pictures of the newest addition to the Johnson family.

"Okay, that's enough," Cyrus said. He stood over his wife, his concerned gaze resting on her strained face.

"Just a few more," Hudson said.

"That's enough," Cyrus said again, this time speaking directly to their spokesperson. "My wife needs to rest, just like my son is doing. You have plenty of pictures. You should be able to find something usable among all of those."

Hudson nodded. "All right, let's go." He waved his hand in a circle above his head and the three who'd arrived with him started packing up. "You're fine with the statement I'll be releasing?" he asked Cyrus.

"Yes, that's fine."

Within seconds, they were gone.

"We're going to leave, too," Trenton said. He walked over to Alannah and put an arm around her shoulders. "Congratulations you two."

"I'll come with you," Ivy said.

They all said their goodbyes, and they left Constance, Cyrus, Daniella, and baby Michael in the room.

"I'm surprised they didn't name the baby Cyrus," Alannah said, as they waited at the elevator.

"I'm not," Trenton said.

"Me either," Ivy added.

"Really? I thought for sure that there'd be a Cyrus the third."

"There's a lot of responsibility attached to the name Cyrus Johnson," Trenton said. The elevator doors slid open and the three of them entered the cab. "I think he wanted to give his son some different choices."

****

Trenton let himself into Alannah's townhouse. His nephew was seven days old, and he and Alannah had gone by the house to see Daniella and the baby. Afterward, they'd gone their separate ways to run errands, and Trenton had stopped at home to shower and change into the long-sleeved shirt and navy slacks he wore under his coat.

On the way to the stairs, Angel rushed out of her cage and trotted over to him.

He bent down and patted her head. "Hey there, Angel. How're you doing, girl?" She let out an excited bark and turned in a circle. Tail wagging, she bounced up on her hind legs and looked up at him expectantly.

"I can't play with you all night," he said, rubbing the dog's head and around her ears. "Your mommy and I are going to The Underground."

Trenton left the Yorkie and climbed the stairs two at a time. As he neared the open bedroom door, he heard "Vivrant Thing" by Q-Tip playing. He came to a stop in the doorway. Even with her out-of-rhythm dancing, Alannah still looked sexy as she applied the finishing touches of her makeup.

Tonight she wore a white Donna Karan blouse with a deep vee neckline. With her small breasts, there was no cleavage, and a thin white gold necklace settled on her chest. High-waisted black trousers and black shoes with a short heel completed the outfit.

No more pretending that high heels were her thing. She told him she admired women who wore them, but admitted they hurt her feet and she had to concentrate too much when she walked. She'd save them for special occasions.

He'd opened accounts for her at several high-end stores, and she'd taken Terri shopping with her. After the trip, she'd made a big deal of expressing how much she appreciated his generosity, which he found amusing. Based on the bills he'd received, she hadn't spent much. He'd bought her gifts before, but he suspected it would take time for her to get used to having him give her gifts as a lover.

Overwhelmed by his love for her, he walked over and pulled her into his arms. He kissed her, hard.

"You're going to kiss off all my lipstick," she muttered, kissing him back and flicking her tongue over his mouth.

"You don't have more?" He reclaimed her lips, drinking from their sweetness and savoring the texture of their lushness.

"I do, but…" She kissed him.

"Okay, then." He kissed her again.

They kissed and kissed, and their mouths devoured each other. His lips moved down to her neck. "Should I give you a hickie?"

"Don't you dare." She slapped his arm and twisted to face the mirror again.

Trenton folded his hands over her stomach and watched her reapply her lipstick. "Did you get through with your application?"

Alannah had decided to get a master of science in molecular biosciences to increase her chances for advancement in her field.

"Almost. I'm waiting on one more recommendation to come in before I submit it."

"We're going to have to spend every night together from now until you start classes. Once you start, you won't have much time between studying and work."

"Every night?" Alannah looked at him in the mirror, amusement in her eyes.

"Yes, every night." He pulled her tight against him so she could feel his rising erection. "Don't you want to wake up next to this every morning?"

"That's not what I'm worried about." She brought a hand to his face and rubbed his cheek. "I hope I don't get tired of seeing your ugly mug every day."

"Funny, I was just thinking the same thing about you."

"Oh really?"

"Yeah, really."

"Meanie." She twisted in his arms and gave him a quick peck on the lips.

Trenton placed a moist kiss to the skin exposed by the revealing neckline and growled. He lifted his head and sighed heavily. "We better get out of here before I have you naked and we never leave."

"Would that be so terrible?" she teased.

"Yes, it would. I already texted the frat that I'd be there, so I want to keep my promise."

Devin had broached the topic of he, Trenton, and another frat brother opening clubs like The Underground in Atlanta, Georgia and Charlotte, North Carolina, where Devin had contacts.

"You ready?" he asked.

"Almost." Alannah scurried over to a table in the corner and turned off the music. With a happy grin on her face, she placed her hand in his. "Ready."

****

They walked into The Underground holding hands. Whenever Trenton stopped and spoke to anyone, he continued to hold Alannah's hand, or left an arm around her waist. Even when he greeted other women, he didn't let her go, giving them one-armed hugs so he could maintain his hold on her.

Alannah didn't shrink back like she used to. In fact, she stuck out her hand first and introduced herself, smiling and making direct eye contact.

They eventually made their way to their reserved table and sat together listening to the musicians before he was called away to the bar. He excused himself and left her alone, planning to wrap up the meeting as soon as possible.

He, Devin, and their frat brother discussed the particulars of the club and the potential spots in each city where they could open them. Trenton would put up the majority of the money.

"Sounds good, but of course I'll need to see everything in writing, like when we opened this place," he said.

Devin nodded. "Of course. Wanted to make sure you were

interested first. We'll put a plan together over the next few weeks."

"Perfect."

They all shook hands.

Trenton's other frat brother looked in the direction of where he'd been sitting with Alannah. "Hey, isn't that you, man?"

Trenton's eyes traveled to the table, and he saw a man bent over, speaking to Alannah. She shook her head and smiled politely, but he didn't give up. He whispered in her ear again, hand braced on the back of her chair, standing way too close.

Trenton tensed, wanting to barge over there and tell the guy to get the hell away from her, but he held fast. She laughed, shook her head again, and the guy finally left.

She lifted her gaze, and when she saw him looking, she smiled and gave a little wave. The tension left his body. He was the luckiest man in the world, and he knew it.

She belonged to him. Not in an archaic, proprietary way, but as part of a whole. They belonged to each other. Always had.

He smiled back at her and answered his frat brother's question truthfully and without reservation.

"Yeah, that's me."

The End

More Stories by Delaney Diamond

Hot Latin Men series
The Arrangement
Fight for Love
Private Acts
Second Chances
Hot Latin Men: Vol. I (print anthology)
Hot Latin Men: Vol. II (print anthology)

Hawthorne Family series
The Temptation of a Good Man
A Hard Man to Love
Here Comes Trouble
For Better or Worse
Hawthorne Family Series: Vol. I (print anthology)
Hawthorne Family Series: Vol. II (print anthology)

Love Unexpected series
The Blind Date
The Wrong Man
An Unexpected Attraction
The Right Time (coming soon)

Johnson Family series
Unforgettable
Perfect
Just Friends
The Rules (coming soon)

Bailar series (sweet/clean romance)
Worth Waiting For

Short Stories
Subordinate Position
The Ultimate Merger

Free Stories
www.delaneydiamond.com

About the Author

Delaney Diamond is the USA Today Bestselling Author of sweet, sensual, passionate romance novels. Originally from the U.S. Virgin Islands, she now lives in Atlanta, Georgia. She reads romance novels, mysteries, thrillers, and a fair amount of nonfiction. When she's not busy reading or writing, she's in the kitchen trying out new recipes, dining at one of her favorite restaurants, or traveling to an interesting locale. She speaks fluent conversational French and can get by in Spanish.

Enjoy free reads and the first chapter of all her novels on her website. Join her e-mail mailing list to get sneak peeks, notices of sale prices, and find out about new releases.

www.delaneydiamond.com

CPSIA information can be obtained
at www.ICGtesting.com
Printed in the USA
BVHW030155261219
567829BV00001B/62/P